BUFFALO SHORTS

A collection of short stories by eight
Western New York authors,
cleverly disguised as a fashion statement.

Adam Paterson

Jeffrey Albert

Mark Donnelly, PhD

Mason Winfield

Ken JP Stuczynski

Austin Clark

Avi Albert

David Kelly

RPSS Publishing - Buffalo, New York

This book is dedicated to
a creative city
bursting with imagination

CONTENTS

Welcome to Buffalo Shorts

A collection of short stories by eight Western New York authors

This may sound like the setup for a joke: A professor, a ghost hunter, an architect, a web designer, and an author walk into a bar.

But instead of a snappy punchline, you receive this anthology of short stories that's part literary experiment, part fever dream, and equal parts wit, mystery, and pure storytelling. Together, it's proof that when wildly different minds collide, the explosion is somehow readable.

These stories, written by a curious collection of eight long-suffering Bills fans, were penned with love, sarcasm, caffeine, and a generous serving of creative panic. Each one was forged in the fires of imagination, tempered in the caverns of self-doubt, and finally published because—let's be honest—we had a deadline.

This collection may be longer than the average therapy session. Still, it's shorter than the Terms and Conditions you pretended to read last week. Think of it as a sampler platter and the literary equivalent of fun-sized candy bars.

So grab a bookmark and adult beverage, dim the lights (unless you're easily spooked), and step into the worlds we've built. You'll discover things you didn't know, witness stuff you can't explain, and meet characters you might actually invite to dinner. Well… perhaps some of them.

Welcome to our book.

Turn the page and plunge headfirst into the tailgate buffet we've created.

It only gets weirder from here.

FACT
FACT
FACT
FACT

FOR SCIENCE!

by Adam Patterson

Lee knew to never wish upon a black hole, unfortunately, Thomas did not. Upon gazing into the void a year ago, he birthed an event that was coming to a culmination the moment the sun set. For now, all have gone to their bed and the night has become too quiet. And pregnant. Yes, it was quiet and pregnant, waiting to give birth to chaos in the small town of Beldovia, New York. Nestled between Rochester and Buffalo, New York, on nights like this, you could hear a low hum and sheepish flaps of white lab coats scurrying around like mice in a barn. It is that flapping that brough the black SUVs that were now crisscrossing the street, their flashing lights were off and their sirens silent, hunting.

In the Southeast corner of the hamlet was a quarter mile fenced in area that was home to an old NIKE site that was the first line of defense to stop any ICBM rockets during the height of the Cold War. Over the years, the site was home to a number of small businesses and government contracts, and currently housed a non-legal university for astrophysics complete with a converted water tower that was now a radio telescope designated BLATS (Beldovia Linear Astronomy Terrestrial System). The two-story box building that covered the top had no markings, no signage, was the town's benefactor, and was more secret than Mrs. Tesco's Brown Butter Cookie recipe, more on her later.

In the fourth sub basement, aptly named - B3, in room 43, hunched over the first computer was Doctor Thomas Yi Simmons, PhD, MD, PMP, single. He squinted, his eyes looking at words like telemetry and frequency. The radio kicked over from a commercial to an interrupting newsflash that NOVA (National Ocean Viewing Agency) for retired fishermen, was being defunded, the last bastion of accepted science. It didn't matter, the object was in range of the BLATs. He directed the array and listened.

The computer lit up as it hit the 21-century line, frequency 1420.4 megahertz, a message was received. the EIQ scale printed out. Thomas grabbed the sheet of paper and looked at its repeating line of EQ IJ5 over 6. His eyes glossed and fists clenched as he grabbed a hold of the wall next to him, tightening his breath. He pulled two short exhales out before taking a deep breath in. He put two fingers on the base of his neck and rubbed.

He looked at his instruments again, "Lee" he shouted. "I need a verification!"

Lee pulled his eyes from a Doppler image of 5I/BLATS, the object Thomas's array was pointed at. It was a long, flat, and a concave object 10 miles long, skirting past Jupiter on a direct course to Earth. Lee ran over and pulled the sheet from Thomas's hand, looking at the same code EQ IJ5 and grabbed his shoulders eyes welling up with tears.

Thomas stiffened, Lee held out his hand to shake. It was a known gesture. Touch was unnatural. Thomas needed Lee, so he clasped his hand, and vigorously obliged. There was a knock at the door. They looked at one another; it must be their lab assistant Halvarti coming back from a wireless transmission of electricity through the crystalline granite structures demonstration.

It didn't open. The two scientists heard whispers from outside the wooden frame. "The voice was not verified." A distinct voice whispered, "This is the 5th door," then there was a long pause and the sound of somebody sucking air from the side of their mouth before the latch made a sharp beep and unlocked.

Thomas looked up and saw a tall, hulking man and young woman dressed in black, guns drawn, with sunglasses on, and masks up. "Hands up" they yelled.

Thomas straightened, "That's not the password," he said. The two officers ran up to the scientists, as Lee screamed, "Who are you!?"

Thomas already knew who it was; they were FACTs (Force Action Correctional Team).

Thomas quickly took the sheet from Lee's hand and hid it in his pocket beneath his lab coat as the officers grabbed Lee and him, pulling them into the hallway. Before them was a polished young Lieutenant with FACT embroidered above their right breast pocket. Pulling out a long receipt like sheet, they started reading: "Under provision 483, which will be passed this evening, you are hereby arrested for the following reasons…" Thomas glanced down the hallway to see other FACT agents opening doors and quietly bringing people out into the hallway.

Lee looked over at his mentor and pointed their eyes to Thomas's pocket before proclaiming, "For science!" With that, Lee crouched down and jammed his shoulder into the officer who was loosely holding Thomas. The good doctor slipped and started running. A chemist from Room B7 took advantage of the commotion, reaching into her pocket and pulling a series of tubes out, screamed "For science!" throwing them to the ground, creating a sticky and slippery substance that expanded and oozed down the hall. The FACT officers all stepped back drawing their weapons. "Watch out!" an officer yelled.

The lieutenant addressed their troops "Cover your ears and repeat your mantras!" The officers were muttering to themselves. "The moon landing was fake," "coincident is proof," "They are all sheep, I'm the free thinker," was heard quietly through the halls. As they regrouped, weapons at the ready, each patted the tin foil safety blanket they kept in their pocket.

Thomas ran to the end where there was a large red button, and hit it, yelling "Swiss Contingency." All the doors in the area opened up, and the panicked rustling of scientists could be heard in each lab, scurrying and keyboards resounded. FACT officers redeployed as reinforcements poured through the stairwell, climbing over the now solidified chemical material. Doctors, rats, and robots ran out of the various rooms throughout the hallways holding external hard drives, each staring at Thomas as he ran screaming, repeating 'Swiss Contingency.' They had 20 minutes to bring their data on hard drives to the basement to be sent in an old NIKE missile up to a satellite where it would dock and transmit to a secure facility in Switzerland, or plug in any gapped servers, whereas the same could be transmitted.

The laboratory assistants ran out and screamed "For science," as they ran toward the FACT officers, yelling uncomfortable phrases like "Science is a process, not an answer," and "We don't actually know what happens after death," and "Pluto is not a planet." Others started yelling out statistics, "The galaxy moved through space at 1.3 million miles per hour," and "The Universe if 13.8 billion years old," while one unhinged assistant shrieked "Time doesn't exist!" making an older FACT officer start to cry.

The FACT officers we're tackling each lab assistant one by one. Most would start with "my aunt, a friend, or a cousin's friend who…" while cuffing each foolhardy Ph.D. student neutralizing their attacks.

Thomas knew that everyone would be rushing to the basement to secure their payloads. He pulled up his lab phone and started his AI interface, securing a connection. He opened up his camera, pulled the paper from his pocket, and took a picture of the data while running up to the surface. Among the commotion he said "Chat, encrypt this data and send it to McMurdo Antarctica."

The AI prompted the parameters of the encryption. Thomas screamed "Highest level of encryption, the data must be protected at all costs!"

The AI answered: "Data is encrypted" and displayed a key with a line through it. "Encryption key thrown away."

"No, it must be available to all the scientists!" Thomas said.

"Invalid parameters. Data is now protected from all parties. Data is locked for all time." The AI reminded him.

Thomas threw his phone to the wall. He burst from the stairwell and arrived at the main entrance. The front was surrounded by black SUV's and sedans with people in lab coats and officers' uniforms bouncing against one another in an uncontrolled chain reaction.

Thomas ran into a FACT officer and instinctively pushed her away, but she grabbed his hand and turned. She reached for her gun, but Thomas was too quick and punched her in the face. He saw the weapon on her waist and grabbed it. The cops all around saw the altercation and began closing in. He pulled the officer close and put the gun up to her head. "He's using science!" Someone shouted and they all backed away.

Thomas and his hostage exited the building, "Your kind will never win." The woman said.

"I have information that will change the course of history!" Thomas exclaimed.

"That's what all scientists say. You're pathetic."

"But, this time it's true!" Thomas said.

"You people have been saying that since 1742 and look what it gave us… more work and less time."

"I can't fix trust with facts…" Thomas sighed. "You just have to believe me."

Most of the scientists were cuffed with zip ties on the ground. Officers were gathering large groups of Ph.D. students and assistants into unmarked buses. Thomas knew the game was up.

He lowered his gun, and the officer turned, grabbing him by his collar. "You will no longer undermine society; you will no longer accelerate change." She remarked as she puffed out her righteous chest.

The earth started to shake as a large NIKE missile crashed through the ceiling of the large box building. The Swiss Contingency was alive, and Thomas knew it wasn't over. Everyone looked up at the fiery plume, it invigorated his colleagues as he saw several yelling "Science!" and using the force of levers to break their zip ties. A cohort of lab coats burst from the main doors throwing chemical concoctions, it was at this moment, they realized there weren't enough FACTs to stop science. and the line of resistance broke free.

In the confusion, Thomas pushed the officer down and jumped to the nearest SUV, jumping into the driver's seat, and pushed the start button. Invalid password blinked on the heads up display. The doctor thought for a minute gazing up on the chaos in front. "Climate change is a hoax" he said. The SUV started up.

Thomas pulled out his personal phone and called around to the other non legal universities and labs, but no one was picking up. It must have been a coordinated attack, he thought. He turned left, right, left, right, straight, he sped up.

Thomas slowed the SUV as he saw flashing red and blue light ahead, a check point. He yanked off his white coat, and threw his glasses to the side. He unbuttoned his collar and pulled his tie before rolling down his window.

"Evening." He said in a calm tone.

They were two state police officers, both on the ready, with their hands inching towards their hips. "Evening. FACT officer" They said slowly. "What brings you out here?" He looked down. "Government plate?"

The other officer was making their way around to the back of the nondescript vehicle. "We raided a non legal science facility and are just cleaning up…" Thomas started. The officer looked down from Thomas's collar onto a white plastic fold that was his pocket protector with his name and title in gold lettering scrolled across.

The officer pulled his gun and Thomas extended his foot, pressing the acceleration.

"Careful! The officer screamed to his compatriots "Watch out, he's not FACT and has science guns!"

The SUV gunned down the road splattering bugs across the windshield hightailing it as the police pursued kicking up a trail of asphalt across the old road. Thomas ran the address book in his head, crossed off any obvious choices, and just as his mind started dwelling on places that start with T, he saw the entrance sign for Dunbrass College and took a sharp left.

The SUV rocked back and forth as it hit pothole after pothole from the defunct road. The college's buildings were run down as the school had seen enrollment decrease and funding dry up. The overgrown brush blocked the building signs but he saw the word 'mptuer' and wrenched his vehicle toward the arrow.

He saw light filter through hazy windows in what looked like a Georgian style three story bricked schoolhouse. He slid his car up to the entrance, jumped out, and ran up, throwing his should into the door. The police were 2.4 minutes away from cuffing him by his estimation. Thomas shut the main doors and braced them with a chair as an old man came out in a tweed suit and asked, "Can I help you?"

Thomas could recognize a fellow academic. "The police are after me, I need to scan and send this piece of paper to McMurdo Independent Research Facility or send this on a rocket to Switzerland, whichever is easier." The old man thought for a moment. "Dean Pfeter." He said.

An older woman came out, straightening up at the sight of Thomas who had a sweat ring around his neck extending to mid-chest. "What is going on, John." She said as the old man turned. "It sounds like science." He said mildly.

They looked at each other. There were two loud thuds at the door as blue and red flashing lights blinked in through the windows. Dean Pfeter looked out the window. John, looked over at her. "We did donate out bodies to science…"

She stood up straight, "Follow me." And waved her arms to Thomas. The three made their way to the back of a computer lab as the thuds at the front door became louder and sounded more like splintering than knocking. Pfeter looked at John, "I got it," he said running out, closing the door behind him.

Down the hall, in a large lecture room, the doors flung open and the teacher who was lecturing to a class of about 20 students on the importance of a Y when laying piper over a T stopped mid sentence. "There is an emergency, and we need you to be hostages. I expect compliance." John said.

Back in the lab. The computer slowly booted up and loaded. Pfeter put in her credentials. Invalid, "Caps lock was on." She tried again. Invalid. "Please look away," Thomas did. She hit the show botton. "I hit R instead of T." She typed again. CRASH! The front door gave way and the boots of FACTs could be heard thudding across the front foyer. "They are here! Start the damn computer!" He forcefully whispered and threw his back against the closed lab door bracing it.

From behind the wooden frame Thomas heard:

"Hold! I'm a scientist and I will use science on them!" John's voice boomed.

"I don't see a weapon" an office yelled to their team.

"It's a science gun!" A student yelled back. "Don't come any closer I don't want to die!"

"He's not a scientist." The officer proclaimed. "They are horrible, hairy creatures, barely human anymore."

"Not this scientist." A student said. "This scientist is a monster under his coat."

"That's not even a lab coat!?"

"I'm in." Pfeter said. Thomas ran over with the piece of paper. She looked at what was in his hand; "Oh," Pfeter said, "we have a scanner you can email from over here. We don't need the computer." Thomas screamed and gripped his fingers shut.

"The scientist is in there!" A voice said from outside of the room.

Thomas opened the copier lid, slammed down the paper, and shut the lid, hitting scan on rapid fire. Email: the machine said. He typed fast as the door handled jingled. Thomas finished the .org as the door splintered and he hit send as his body slammed against the machine when the officers burst into the room.

His hands forced behind his back and his head hit the ground and a knee against his spine. "Down." The officer said before yanking him up. Thomas looked back to the light on the machine – "Turn around" the officer said.

Thomas's head was lowered into the car as he looked back at Dunbrass College, the car door shut. Dean Pfeter gave Thomas a thumbs up. John mouthed 'green'. And the good doctor smiled.

MEASURING CLOUDS

by Jeffrey Albert

The field was awash with shades of the color, orange, in and out of focus, it drifted. Fine specks of blue in the field began to shrink...

He took a deep breath.

His heart was beating in time to his gasping inhalations,

Slowly, he became aware of where he was upon awakening.

His breathing returned to normalcy, his heart complied as if on a single wave. The startle reflex faded with the passing of his dream state. Always the same dream. The dream was always a wavering and indistinct awareness within a spectrum of changing colors.

He had tried for years to define, to understand, and even to plumb its meaning.

In return, this dream had teased him, beckoning him endlessly. Nothing could bring it any closer to his satisfaction. 'Clouds,' he had heard her say for the thousandth time as he shifted in a seated posture at the backboard of his tousled bed.

'Still here," he thought. He drew a deep breath and released it down to his toes.

The morning sun warmed him to the point of brightening irritation. He knew he had to get moving. Farnsworth, the grey Tabby, was nowhere. He assumed that his tossing and turning had sent his steadfast friend on the scurry. The cat obliged in moments like these, by confining himself within the shaggy diaphragm of the old boxspring supporting them both. Out of sight, perhaps, but closer than appearances allowed. Farnsworth's breathing could be heard in the silent beachfront house. "Still heeere…" he whispered to himself. A shifting sound occurred from below his mattress. One was not late with Farnsworth, no, it was a timeworn ritual by now.

David was an obsessive type. He had long grown used to the sounds of the pounding surf, the sight of the windblown trees, and the circling mewling gulls and skittering plovers. It was not at all unpleasant and served to create a continuity that had linked him to a source in nature far beyond the endless traffic, banal morning radio programs, and discarded throwaway cups of stinking, cheap coffee. Getting to the picture window in a halting shuffle, David wistfully thought, 'Clouds.'

What was Mykonos like today? 'The same' was his response to himself.

His beachfront house was not an escape exactly. Though his sister, Bertthie, had passed on a long time ago. She was the mystery to him that necessitated his isolation, even now. Their Rust Belt childhood had chased him across the country into every hiding place he could imagine. Here, exhausted, in Monterey, he had finally stopped. He found himself precariously balanced between sea and sky. The adapted shipping container he had designed and constructed, as his residence, had betrayed his transience. Pitched between the blasting, dominating sun and the roiling and tumbling coastline, he had found just enough place to call home. There was nowhere else to turn to. No other domicile had contained him.

At these morning moments, she was closest to him. Her sun-bleached hair and freckled skin had given her the appearance of a child who could never be changed into someone else. She was the brightest of all the siblings who shared the old and shoddy walk-up unit. Their parents had tried everything they could think of, even family therapy, for years. Managing their expectations became full-time work for them. They did not know her at all.

But why? She had nothing to prove at that age. Why did they make themselves so directly responsible for untangling her unpredictability by yoking their expectations upon her? So out of touch with the times, invariably cowed by an irrelevant and immaterial past, WHY HAD THEY DESCENDED UPON HER? She had reason to toss them to the winds. She did not. She would not.

David regarded the morning horizon. The textured ceiling had lost all trace of shadows. The large picture window revealed an unending vista of cerulean sky on one side of the rectangular glass volume of his home. The other side seemed to dangle above a darker Prussian blue ocean. He placed himself between the two opposing directions. It was here that he was most comfortable. There, balancing two conditions. Maybe seeming opposites, but then maybe necessarily complementary. He had come to peace with the notion that the pitching of opposites was life itself. His own life.

The drafting table was also bare. Not a shred of tracing paper was hastily taped over a dozen other inevitably discarded sketches, furiously rendered. His various pencils were put neatly away. The floor was littered with torn images of other failures in yellow tracing paper. Yet he easily worked his way across the brightly lit floor, bypassing rumpled sketches without a sound, intending to wake no one.

This night and morning shuffle was born of old habits. There was no one else to wake up anymore. Mr. Farnsworth might care, the noise often arousing him to dive in shredding mode towards David's bare feet. The sketch papers rattled as David passed. He could hardly imagine seeing the cat today. Farnsworth's dream time was audible within the household silence. Glancing down, David thought the mess was simply unintelligible wads of midnight drawing fervor… ending in nothing.

He stood before the coffee maker. The pans in the sink were dirty. 'Start with coffee…always, coffee.' He smirked at the thought. As he poured the remnants of last night's pot, he felt compelled to sit in the bent plywood seat he had always favored. He no longer fretted about the origins of, the names of, the processes of making. None of the details seemed to settle nor 'alight upon his brow' as they said in jest at the office back then.

He never liked the condescension of the joke. He felt it was a yardstick of their pretensions, the co-workers. They would parade endlessly in troops around his desk. He had long ago learned to hear nothing from their reports. They updated each other continuously to the point of absurd fascination over trivialities that he had no interest in tracking. The more he came to know, the more he intentionally carved himself out from their presence. Then the dreams from childhood had started all over again.

He eased himself into the seat. The cold cup in hand. As the sun climbed, the misty smog of the bay burned away, revealing a rose-tinted sky. It was her, Berttie. She was the artist. The color rose. His eyes closed. Her sunbaked skin and red striped t-shirt. Why had she never listened to anything they had said to her? She had laughed at all the propositions and suppositions made on her behalf. Bertthie had no interest whatsoever in anything they offered. She was not 'lazy', the most oft-shouted epithet placed upon her. She could have ruined them and their reliably off-center remonstrations.

That was Bertthie. She could not be won over by imposition nor by urgent pleas. She made the time to notice things we all missed. Smallish things no one cared about. People, too. Those days were littered with people who seemed to enjoy making loud declarations of abilities they uniquely possessed. 'Le Cicerone'. David remembered seeing the painting series in New York, Madrid, and Brussels with Louisa, his partner during college. She thought the work meaningless, a fantasy.

The work by René Magritte, which displayed the bombast of the self-anointed ones, deeply affected David, however. A mute cannon-mouthed Cicero. The bastion of rebellion in a collapsing anti-historic time. Rome was falling, with no memory. Cicero was made mute forever. He was displayed in antique costume while trumpeting in a crooked piazza in the first painting David ever saw. A scene with a prominent pedestal of nothing, found nowhere and for no one. Blasts of fire as the flame of time, promising riches and bringing a silent end to the ceremony instead, blazed across one of the canvases he saw in Belgium. Odd thoughts ran through his mind at each exhibit that they attended.

The very last painting, at the last exhibit they had attended together in Paris, 'Voice of Silence,' made him stop. Louisa laughed as he stood still. She smilingly ran into an adjacent room. He saw the large, multi-colored canvas she was heading for. Lost in thought, he followed her without a word. From that day onward, he could see the possibility of pure abstraction rendered as reality. The paintings had shaken him after all these years. He wondered how Magritte could depict such a place. How had he seen those airless places? Had the painter heard the echoing sounds descend into a vast void to be lost forever? His drafting board loomed before him. David's reverie of the past had receded quickly as a written schedule and deadline loomed visibly in his notes.

David quaffed the cold coffee. A splay of white vapor wisps washed across the morning sky. The ocean moisture had risen in the general heat of the day and formed above his house.

'She was the artist, she could see.' David thought after a quick gulp. He winced at the surprisingly bitter taste. 'She could teach others how to see…' His thoughts trailed away. He knew he would be nowhere near here if it were not for her. The sky grew thicker as he sat.

'Clouds' What were they? David once asked her.

Bertthie had said to him in reply. 'Clouds are what you cannot take away, what you cannot grasp. They are moved by some sweet will of their own.'

Still in school at the time. It was on one of those timeless and aimless days for which David still longed. They both stood on an open hilltop, under a vast expanse of blue sky. The valleys below them were covered in Black-Eyed Susans, Milkweed, Lupine, and Shasta Daisies. 'God knows what else.' David was momentarily embarrassed to hear himself say it out loud, involuntarily. Instantly, he was silent again. He had always known that he had been here in this field with her. A part of him had never left her on that day. David remembered that Bertthie, in a flush of emotion, had only smiled as he gasped at the unfolding vista. She had brought him here. She had said to David that she had seen the place in her dreams. That was when she had grabbed him from his homework desk and had driven them both there in her battered Nova. That was decades ago. That was far away.

He had gone away from home soon afterward. Within his first year, he met Luisa at a small Manhattan art college. She was dark-haired, serious, and fiery. He understood her very well and that she could not be reasoned with. She was his confidant. She answered no one's command. She could get him to move and move quickly anywhere on earth. It was exhilarating. He had completely forgotten his past. A sea of lights, long nights, and deep, pulsating music enveloped him during his time with her. He was in a spell that unrolled before him.

The wish to be near her took him to places he had never dreamed of. He was soon welcomed in cities he had only read about in old and rarely read books. The yellow cards in the rear pockets bore only a few names of borrowers of these books after 50 years. David learned to love the moments he was alone with these books.

Louisa, mad for it all, reaching past words, pulled David from his habitual hiding place in the musty stacks of the central library. She would find the places where he and his work would shine. She skillfully led David unto the ends of the earth. He could barely catch or even organize himself while arriving at each new vista Louisa had taken him to. He was surprised to learn that each time, she had the plans well thought out. David was covered, always.

After a few years, that was it, an ending, maybe unlike his sister and their parents. He just could not hear Luisa anymore. Was he exhausted? Yes. Yes and no. But in any case, she was gone. Gone forever, he felt. There was nothing left of him by the time he crawled into his present home. To recover? He thought hard.

When he awoke again, having drifted off into sleep at the drafting table, pencil in hand, the surf was louder. The afternoon sun had begun to quietly descend on the horizon. He felt uncomfortable. The last time he had seen Bertthie was the last time anyone had seen her. Why had it happened? No one could say. He kissed her goodbye as they arrived at La Guardia again. Bertthie was living at home at that time. She was different. There had been so many heated exchanges between her and their parents about her future that he was not surprised to see her looking downcast as he looked back at her. Luggage at the curb, he regarded the shrinking car as it entered a voluminous stream of mad traffic. 'This is it…' was all he could say to himself. Pulling his shoulders up to carry the baggage, he noticed she was long gone. He had learned the meaning of lost hope in a New York Minute.

As he got back to class and to Luisa, he could think only of Bertthie. What had she been trying to tell him? The only interest he took in this, his last semester, was in a lecture about, of all subjects, the process of dimensioning. Of measuring infinitesimal space and making it clear enough that one could construct a three-dimensional world from it. But that was not the most interesting portion of the lecture. The professor was speaking about the process of creating. How the impetus to embody and realize creation was not a mechanical gesture like other professors there seemed to preach. There was a process by which one might, literally, dimension space from memory and be unrestricted by time, if only one could enter the field. The field of pure potentiality.

David had mulled over that notion endlessly. What on earth could that be? Why do we call it a process at that stage? He started trying to map his thinking to vainly gain access to that state.

But with Luisa, he remembered being thrilled to be pulled away time and time again. One thousand nights awaited him.

So here he was. Now there was the night spread out before him with twinkling lights in the vast distance. The house seemed small tonight. The light from within the house made his creation feel like a cage again. The luminaires shining against the walls and windows in the dark defined the space, confining him. The ocean wind blew darkly across his table, bringing the smells of drying wood and sea brine directly to him. David knew he would dream deeply again.

As he sat preparing to see Sarah, another friend, this time, an actual friend, he remembered Berttie's last words to him:

'Look for me there, while you are away…' was all he remembered. She had pointed to the western horizon in a gesture that had puzzled David at the time.

David got up and drew the shades of the living room. He opened a can for Farnsworth, who had been mewling at his feet all the while. He tossed his windbreaker over his right shoulder and quickly departed into the deep blue night, which had so suddenly dropped upon him.

LAKE
EFFECT,
BABY

THE LEGEND OF SHORT-SLEEVE STAN AND TWO-COAT MARIA

by Mark Donnelly, PhD.

They call him Short-Sleeve Stan, which is a misnomer because the sleeves are rarely the story. The story is his legs–blinding, stubborn, winter-proof legs that stride through Buffalo like the city owes them money. In January he is a migrating lighthouse, a human icicle in cargo shorts, calves defiant as snowbanks. In February he is a public service announcement for hypothermia. In March–when the rest of Buffalo says, "Eh, could go either way"–he's already switched to the "summer shorts" with the extra pocket for a Lloyd Taco.

He has a system. Shorts and boots if there's more than six inches of snow; shorts and sneakers if it's light and fluffy; shorts and sandals if the sun appears for more than eleven minutes or someone on TV says the word "thaw." His mother used to call him "my little space heater." His father just sighed, handed him a shovel, and said, "If you're gonna dress like a fool, you might as well be a useful fool."

Here is how the legend began.

The Lore of the Calves

Stan's calves are not normal calves. They are the result of a childhood spent shoveling driveways so long the horizon had horizons. He grew up on the East Side near the kind of corner where everybody has a cousin who once served Rick James coffee at a Tim Hortons. The block was tight-knit, loud, and unfazed by weather. Snow came sideways, diagonally, from underneath; wind bent at ninety degrees and took your hat off just to show you who's boss. Stan learned to respect the wind by outrunning it.

By high school he was the kid who'd run to Mighty Taco in a blizzard for a class party, come back with tacos still hot and eyebrows frosted like a Christmas cookie. By college he was that guy at UB who wore shorts to class because "the lecture hall is basically Florida if you sit in the top row." And by his early twenties he was a fixture at Bills games: shirtless from November through playoffs (when the playoffs existed, hypothetically), chest painted, lips blue–not from paint but from the meteorological realities of Orchard Park.

He wasn't just shirtless. He was shirtless with artistry. He painted slogans. "NO PANTS, NO PROBLEM." "LAKE EFFECT, BABY." "WARMTH IS A MINDSET." Once he painted a full map of Erie County across his chest and labeled Orchard Park as "NIPPLE #1" and the other side "NIPPLE #2." The TV broadcast wouldn't show it, but he gained a little local fame. People would elbow their friends: "That's the shorts guy."

He loved it. He loved being the walking dare of Buffalo. He loved saying, "There's no such thing as cold weather, just inappropriate clothing." He loved that feeling of the stadium wind blasting over the upper deck and cutting right through everyone else like a knife through sponge candy… while he stood there grinning, balanced on a folding table, preparing to body-slam his way into certain orthopedic bills. The Bills Mafia credo: through tables we become one.

And then he met Maria.

Two-Coat Maria

Maria grew up on the West Side, a neighborhood rhythm of church bells, porch stories, nosy Aunties, and Sunday sauce. She had black curly hair, a laugh that could start a rave, and a coat collection so extensive her closet sounded like a parade of geese every time she opened it. She had a rule: "I dress for the weather I have, not the weather I wish for." If the weatherman said "lake effect," she said, "Okay but from which lake and at what velocity?"

They met in line at Wegmans because of a rotisserie chicken. It was the last one, shimmering under heat lamps like a small sun. They reached for it at the same time. He had frost on his eyelashes; she had a scarf around her face like a spy. The chicken purred quietly, warm, decisive. They negotiated.

"You take the top half," he said. "I'll take the drumsticks."

"That's not how chickens work," she said, smiling with her eyes.

He offered a compromise: "We could share it. I got Labatt at home."

She appraised the shorts, the purpling knees, the socks that said "GO BILLS" in a font invented by maniacs. She studied his face, which was handsome in a small-dog-at-the-window kind of way–eager, fearless, possibly in danger. "Are you cold?" she asked.

He shook his head too quickly. "I haven't been cold since 2014."

"Why 2014?"

"The day I stopped believing in sleeves."

"That's not a year, that's a cry for help."

They split the chicken anyway. They watched the Sabres lose in overtime and the Bills win in the fourth, and by dessert they were arguing over who had the better Beef on Weck: Schwabl's or Charlie the Butcher. He told her she had the most beautiful laugh he'd ever heard in subarctic conditions. She told him he had admirable knees for someone who clearly lacked self-preservation.

A month later they were inseparable. They went to Niagara Falls and judged the tourists' footwear. They took long drives down to Hamburg, stopping at any yard sale that had a box labeled "mystery cables." They bought a snowblower together and named it "The Shovelizer." He showed her how to save a parking spot with a cracked lawn chair; she showed him the proper way to salt steps so your mailman doesn't sue you.

And of course, they went to Bills games. He without a shirt, shorts glowing like a warning sign, chest painted with block letters: WE BELIEVE. She bundled, ballooning out into a mobile couch, handing him hand warmers like communion.

"Just try a coat," she said sometimes.

"I can't hear you over the sound of my freedom," he would reply, which earned a glare and a thermos of chili.

But love is patient. Love is kind. Love, however, eventually writes ultimatums on stationery with little snowflakes.

The Pants Ultimatum

It happened in late November, two days after a lake-effect event that buried a school bus so deeply they briefly considered turning it into student housing. The city was still digging out. There were cars shaped like whales. Neighbors waved to each other from tunnels carved between the porch and the world.

Maria came over with a casserole, an extra shovel, and an expression that meant business. She set the casserole down, opened her bag, and took out a folded stack like she was deploying a parachute.

"Stan," she said, "we need to talk about your life choices. Specifically, from the waist down."

He glanced at the stack. It was pants. They were handsome—dark denim, a pair of flannel-lined khakis, a pair of something with stretch that looked like a compromise between adulthood and stubbornness. They radiated warmth. He recoiled like a vampire in a garlic boutique.

"Maria," he said slowly, "I appreciate your passion, but pants and I… we don't mix."

"You don't mix with pants, or pants don't mix with you?"

"Mutual incompatibility."

"What if I told you my mother would never sign off on our wedding unless you show up in pants."

He blinked. The word "wedding" had entered the conversation like a To Be Continued sign. He loved Maria. He had been carrying around a ring for weeks, waiting for the right moment–maybe the big screen, maybe at the top of the City Hall observation deck, maybe spelled out in salt on a pristine driveway.

He cleared his throat. "Hypothetically, were I to propose, are you saying there's a… a pant clause?"

"There's a long pants clause," she said. "For the ceremony. For the photos. For the sake of my Nana, who fainted in 1989 when a cousin wore white socks with a tux and still mentions it every Thanksgiving."

Stan pictured it: him in a tuxedo, the weight of fabric hugging his legs like two small, polite bears. He felt itchy in places that didn't even exist. "I… I don't know if I can."

Maria put a hand on his arm. "I love you because you're you," she said. "But I need you alive and frostbite-free. I need to know you can bend for the things that matter to us. Pants aren't just pants. They're a symbol."

"Of oppression."

"Of compromise."

He looked at the pants. The pants looked back, taciturn, undefeated. Buffalo wind moaned across the windows, testing seals, rattling old drafts awake. Somewhere a plow bellowed like a dinosaur.

"Okay," he said finally. "If I can prove to you that pants are unnecessary, can we revisit the clause?"

"How would you possibly prove that?"

He shrugged. "Science."

The Scientific Method of Stupidity

His plan, in retrospect, was poor. He decided to take part in the Polar Plunge fundraiser at Woodlawn Beach… in February… shirtless, obviously, and in shorts, double obviously… and emerge not only alive but cheery, thereby demonstrating that his blood was essentially wing sauce and he felt neither hot nor cold, only righteous.

Maria, because love is a co-signer on loans to chaos, agreed—with conditions. "You will have medical personnel present," she said. "You will warm up afterward. And if you so much as turn a shade I can't find in a crayon box, you put on these." She held up the flannel-lined khakis.

They went with friends. The shoreline looked like a bouncer had iced down Lake Erie for a keg. A guy dressed as a chicken yelled, "LET'S GO!" A woman in a red tutu stared at the horizon like it owed her money. The wind announced itself as Mr. January. Stan bounced in place, pumped up, refusing hand warmers like little traitors.

Maria kissed him, hard, like a stamp. "Come back alive, dummy," she said.

The horn blew. Stan sprinted. The water met him like a lawsuit. He didn't scream—he whooped, the sound of a man in the exact center of his legend. He plunged, he rose, he flexed, he ran back out as if pursued by the ghost of every sensible decision he'd never made.

And then he turned purple. Not all at once, but his knees went eggplant, his thigh a startling shade of egg yolk, and his calves a marbled pattern known to naturalists as "buffoon camouflage." He shook. His teeth attempted Morse code: SOS.

Maria wrapped him in towels, in blankets, in mercy. She gave him hot chocolate. He drank it like it had rent money. When he could speak, he whispered, "I'm fine."

She held up the flannel-lined khakis like a sheriff with a warrant. "Say the words."

He glared, a gladiator facing pants. He glanced at the paramedic, who nodded "bro" in a language beyond words. He sighed and nodded, sliding one leg, then the other, into the warm cave of adulthood.

Reader, they were… nice. They were warmth as an argument. He could feel his soul climb back into his body. He hated that he liked it. He scowled at Maria, who arched an eyebrow so lovingly it might as well have been a hug.

"Pants aren't poison," she said. "Sometimes they're a hug."

He pointed a shaky finger. "This changes nothing about my game-day policy."

"Sure," she said, and didn't wink, but her tone winked on her behalf.

The Proposal *(and the Uninvited Pants)*

Stan planned it perfectly. Bills vs. Dolphins, December, snow globe game, national TV. He had a sign: MARIA, WILL YOU MARRY ME? (YES = THROW PANTS). He coordinated with their whole section, with the guy who dressed as a ketchup bottle, with the woman who always wore a cape made of old Bills jerseys. He told the camera guy whose cousin knew his cousin's barber's dog walker.

At halftime he would stand on the back of the seats, shirtless, shorts dangeling in the gale, and raise the sign. The camera would pan. The stadium would roar. Pants would rain down in ceremonial rejection.

Maria suspected something. She wore her warmest coat and her second-warmest ring finger. Her mother and Nana were "mysteriously" in the same section, pretending they had won tickets on the radio. The snow was that holiday-movie snow, fat and forgiving, gilding even the port-a-potties with grace.

Second quarter. Josh Allen did something physics teachers would have questions about. The place vibrated. Stan squeezed Maria's hand. He was nervous in a way that had nothing to do with temperature. Halftime came. The marching band skidded in little festive ways. The camera guy gave him a look: Now.

Stan rose. He lifted the sign… which promptly caught the wind and nearly carried him to Canada. He wrestled it down. The camera found him. The Jumbotron found him. The world found him: there he was, ShortSleeve Stan, shirtless among the snow, shorts declaring their sovereignty.

MARIA, WILL YOU MARRY ME?

Maria's hands flew to her mouth. She laughed that laugh that starts parades. The section screamed. Someone threw a Zubaz scarf like a flag. And then—because the universe has a sense of humor—a row behind them a man yelled, "YES! MARRY HIM, BUT PUT ON PANTS!" and launched a pair of sweatpants like a catapult.

They hit Stan in the face. The Jumbotron froze on Stan whacked by pants, then cut to a replay like it was a pick-six. The stadium roared like Zeus. Maria doubled over laughing, which is dangerous in thirty-degree wind chill but medically necessary sometimes.

She pulled him close, kissed him, and shouted, "YES!" He lifted her, triumphant, which made the camera do a tasteful slow zoom, which made the announcer say, "Folks, love truly warms the heart," which made every uncle in Buffalo groan and secretly dab a tear.

Later, in the concourse, a stranger slapped his shoulder and said, "Congrats, Pantsless."

Stan grinned. He had a fiancée and a new nickname. He would take both.

Pants Negotiations

Engagement is not just rings and cake tastings. It is logistics, psychology, and relatives. Everyone had an opinion. Uncle Louie said, "Let the boy wear shorts; it's branding." Aunt Patsy said, "If he shows up at church in bare knees I will faint backward into the choir." Nana fingered her rosary and murmured, "Saints preserve us from man-calves in January." Stan's mom said, "I have waited my entire life to see him in slacks."

Maria proposed the Treaty of Trousers, a document both silly and sacred:

1. Groom shall wear long pants on the day of the wedding, the rehearsal dinner, and associated photo appointments.

2. Groom shall be permitted to change into "formal shorts" for the reception after 9:30 p.m., defined as shorts that do not feature cargo pockets large enough to smuggle pierogies.

3. Stadium policy shall continue to be shirtless-in-winter, but groom shall carry emergency thermal leggings for temperatures below "your breath freezes to your eyebrows" on a scale to be mutually agreed upon.

4. All parties shall refrain from public shaming; private roasting permitted with consent.

Stan read it like it was a lease. He glanced at the flannel-lined khakis hanging on the chair. He thought of Maria's Nana, who once slipped him twenty bucks for shoveling a driveway and then said, "Get yourself some pants with this." He thought of the Polar Plunge. He thought of the Jumbotron pants to the face.

He signed.

Maria smiled like a sunrise. "You won't regret this," she said.

"I already do," he said, and kissed her anyway.

Premarital Pantaloon Practice

They went shopping. They learned a language. "Inseam" is a way of measuring shame. "Break" is not what happens to your will; it is where the pant meets the shoe. "Tailoring" is witchcraft.

The tailor was a tiny man named Yusef who had opinions like artillery fire. He clucked at Stan's measurements and whirled a tape around him like a lasso. "You want comfort," Yusef declared. "You want freedom, yes? We can do this. We make pants that feel like you forgot you wearing them."

"That's precisely my ideal," Stan said.

Yusef produced a fabric that felt like a cloud had joined a gym. "Stretch," he said, eyes glinting. "Heat-holding. Breathable. These pants hug you like a grandmother who respects boundaries."

Stan tried them on. He looked in the mirror and did not see a traitor. He saw a guy getting married. He saw Maria's face. He saw himself not as a legend but as a person at the center of a community that would show up with shovels when the forecast turned biblical. He saw room for two things to be true: that he could be the shorts guy and also be the pants guy when required by love and Nana.

He blinked. "Okay," he said, voice rough. "Okay."

Yusef made magic. The tux fit like it had been waiting for him. When he walked, there was a swish that sounded like adulthood. He joked about it: "Hear that? That's the sound of a 401(k)." Maria rolled her eyes and squeezed his hand.

The Wedding Forecast

Buffalo obliged them with weather that could be described as "earnest." It was February because they wanted a winter wedding and off-season venue rates. The morning blew sideways snow. By noon the sun cut through like a grin. By ceremony time the sky had a dramatic pink bruise of sunset, and the church steps were edged with piles of very photogenic snow.

Inside, the heat was festive. Aunt Patsy fanned herself with a program and hissed at anyone who breathed too loud. The organ hummed. The Bills' bye week meant half the congregation wore Bills socks under their formalwear. The florist had tucked tiny blue and red ribbons into the centerpieces, subtle enough that Nana didn't faint.

Stan stood at the altar in pants that did not betray him. He breathed. He looked down occasionally to make sure the pants remained pants and hadn't scampered off. The groomsmen pretended not to watch his legs like a nature documentary.

Then Maria came down the aisle, and all concerns evaporated. She was incandescent. She had tiny snowflakes pinned in her hair and a look that told him she'd hold a shovel with him at 5 a.m. in a whiteout and laugh while doing it. He had to blink hard because his eyelashes had memories of freezing and tried to crisp up in sympathy.

The priest, who was a Bills fan and had a sense of theater, said, "We are gathered here today to celebrate something warmer than a thousand space heaters." People snorted. The vows were beautiful. Maria promised to bring extra gloves in every glove-shaped emergency. Stan promised to wear long pants in "all solemn indoor occasions and any outdoor setting where my kneecaps might distract from the sacrament at hand." The congregation applauded. Nana dabbed her eyes. Aunt Patsy checked his cuffs for socks; they were black and dignified and would not cause a 1989 incident.

They kissed. The church bells rang. Somewhere outside a plow saluted.

Reception, or: The Legend Evolves

At the reception, beneath strings of lights and an enormous banner that read "ALL YOU NEED IS LOVE (AND A RELIABLE SNOWBLOWER)," they danced. He danced like a guy discovering his knees still function with fabric near them. She danced like a person who had successfully negotiated pants with a mythological creature.

At 9:31 p.m., as per treaty, he disappeared and reemerged in formal shorts: navy, tailored, no cargo, hem just above the knee. The DJ announced, "Ladies and gentlemen, we have entered the shorts portion of the evening." The place erupted. Uncle Louie attempted a backflip. A distant cousin yelled, "Show 'em what a Buffalo winter looks like!" and opened a door to the patio, letting in a gust that made the centerpieces lean.

They took photos in the snow: bride in boots under her gown, groom in formal shorts and tux jacket, both holding mugs of hot chocolate, steam haloing like good intentions. The photographer got one favorite: Maria tucking a tiny hand warmer into the pocket of Stan's formal shorts while he looked at her like he'd just learned the word "gratitude."

Toasts happened. The best man told the Polar Plunge story with embellishments (he added a swan and a small Canadian border incident). Maria's sister spoke about compromise and how love is a coat you share. Nana stood, the microphone squealing, and said, "Welcome to the family, Knees," then added, "Okay, sit, you're making me nervous," which made the room roar.

Late in the night, the Bills highlight reel played on a projector: four minutes of miracles and heartbreak, snow swirling across the screen like confetti. Stan and Maria stood hand in hand, and she whispered, "You know, I don't mind the shirtless thing at games."

He grinned. "You're a saint."

"But," she said, "we're bringing the emergency leggings."

"Amen," he said.

Happily Ever After, But With Weather

Married life suited them like a well-fitted parka. They shoveled together in companionable silence, the kind of silence that sounds like love. They adopted a rescue dog named Pinto after Pinto Ron (Kenny Johnson),the patron saint of tailgating. Pinto wore a puffy coat that could stop bullets.

Game days remained an artform. Stan stayed shirtless unless the emergency leggings scale–calibrated with scientific terms like "Nope" and "My Nostrils Froze Shut"–signaled a Level Elsa. He remained shorts committed, but not shorts imprisoned. Sometimes, on the early-morning walk to the coffee shop in February, he'd slip on Yusef's miracle pants, and Maria would pretend not to notice while beaming like a lighthouse.

He became a small local celebrity. Kids at the bus stop would shout, "Shorts Man!" and he'd perform a brief hamstring stretch as if demonstrating proper winter form. News crews put him on B-roll whenever a storm rolled in: a shot of a man in shorts pushing a car out of a snowbank, another of the same man carrying a tray of wings down a sidewalk like a waiter in Antarctica.

And then there was the pants charity.

It started as a joke. After the wedding, they had a pile of novelty pants people had given them: sequined sweatpants, Bills Zubaz with "FORMAL" embroidered sarcastically on the cuff, thermal leggings with little buffalos stamped on them. Maria said, "We should do a fundraiser. Get people to donate winter gear for folks who need it. We'll call it Pants for the People." Stan, who liked a cause as much as he liked a punchline, said, "We can do a lap around Delaware Park in shorts to raise awareness." They did. A hundred people followed, half in shorts, half in normal clothes, all laughing, all lugging bags of coats and pants for shelters.

"Pants for the People" became an annual deal. The first year they filled two trucks. The second year, four. The local news interviewed Maria, who said, "It's not about what you wear; it's about showing up for each other." They interviewed Stan, who, still in shorts, said, "Pants are a metaphor for community," which made the anchor blink like a man who expected a joke and got philosophy.

The Game That Changed the Weather

There was one game that will be told around fire pits for decades. An honest-to-God blizzard, the kind that makes even Buffalo go, "All right, that's enough." The stadium was half-buried. Visibility: two and a half feet. The national media called it "snowmageddon" and sent correspondents who tried to pronounce "Cheektowaga" and failed publicly.

The city did what it does: neighbors dug neighbors out. Strangers pushed strangers' cars. A convoy of snowmobiles helped bring players to the stadium. Maria looked at the emergency leggings scale, which had been updated with a new level: "Legally a Snow Globe." She handed Stan the thermal leggings.

He looked at them, looked at the sky, looked at her hand. He took them. He tugged them on under his shorts. She handed him a hot water bottle like contraband. "Stick it in the back of your shorts," she said.

He did. He waddled like a duck with a secret. They laughed until their cheeks hurt. They trudged to their seats. The people around them cheered when they appeared; somebody held up a sign that read: WE TRUST THE PANTS PLAN.

During the fourth quarter, with snow whipping sideways so hard it sculpted the air, the Jumbotron found them again. Stan, in shorts plus leggings, bare-chested except for the hastily painted words LOVE WINS. Maria beside him, bundled and beaming. They kissed for the camera. The place roared—not at them exactly, but at what they represented: the audacity of joy in a world that sometimes forgets how.

The Bills won on a field goal nobody saw until it was already in the next county. People cried. People hugged. The plows honked a celebratory honk. As the stands emptied, an elderly man, face pink and lined with winters, tapped Stan's arm. "I wore shorts to every game in the '70s," he said, "then I got married. Best trade I ever made."

Stan smiled. "Me too," he said.

The Long View

Years later, kids would tug at Maria's coat: "Mrs. Shorts Man! Tell the Polar Plunge story!" She'd roll her eyes affectionately and tell them the PG version. Stan would be in the yard, brushing snow off the grill–because yes, there is winter grilling and it is a sacred rite–wearing shorts, obviously, and sometimes, quietly, pants.

They'd travel: a trip to Arizona in January where he proclaimed, "I don't even feel it here," and she said, "That's because this is a fake sky," and they laughed until a cactus judged them. A summer trip to the Finger Lakes, where he discovered that pants in ninety degrees are a terrible idea and apologized to everyone who had ever been pantsed by society. A fall pilgrimage to the old family plot in Forest Lawn Cemetery, where they left a tiny pair of baby socks on the headstone of a great-grandfather who'd immigrated with only a hammer and an attitude.

They taught Pinto to fetch hand warmers. They taught their future kids (we're getting ahead of ourselves, but we've all read a story before) to layer. They taught them that love sometimes looks like a hot thermos pressed into cold hands, the steady presence next to you while the wind tests the seams of your life.

On their tenth anniversary, Yusef's shop threw a party–half joke, half genuine. "To my finest challenge," he said, raising a glass. "The man I taught to love pants." Stan toasted back: "To the man who made pants feel like shorts." Maria toasted: "To the man who made shorts feel like home."

Epilogue: The Pants Clause

People sometimes ask Maria if she ever regrets making the pants clause. "Never," she says, eyes bright. "It wasn't about pants. It was about us stepping into something together, even if it felt weird at first."

People sometimes ask Stan if he misses full-time reckless shorts. He grins. "Shorts aren't reckless. Shorts are a lifestyle. But I have expanded my portfolio."

He still wears shorts all winter long. He still goes to Bills games without a shirt, his chest a billboard for hope. But sometimes, when the wind comes in sideways and his eyelashes try to secede, he pulls on the emergency leggings. When Nana is watching, he wears slacks. When Maria's cold, he wraps her in his coat–yes, he owns a coat now; it was quietly acquired and now lives by the door like a faithful dog–and stands between her and the gusts.

You can love someone for exactly who they are and still ask them to be brave in a new way. You can wear shorts in a blizzard and pants to a church and mean both sincerely. You can be the guy who body-slams folding tables in a parking lot and the guy who shows up with soup for the neighbor whose snowblower died. You can be a legend and a partner. You can be warm where it counts.

Buffalo will keep being Buffalo–wind that elbows you, snow that makes architecture of clouds, neighbors who show up, a football team that turns your heart into a drum. Stan and Maria will keep walking into it together: her in sensible boots, him in shorts with a plan B, their breaths writing small white poems in the air.

And sometimes, when the lake howls and the sky turns theatrical and the whole city looks like a cake dusted with sugar, you might spot them on the corner near the Wegmans where it began, arguing cheerfully over the proper amount of horseradish for Beef on Weck. He'll be in shorts, obviously. She'll be in a coat that could double as a tent. He'll nudge her, and she'll nudge back, and as they step into the crosswalk, he'll adjust the cuff of his emergency leggings beneath the hem of his shorts, grinning because compromise, like Buffalo, isn't always pretty, but it's strong as hell.

And that, friends, is how the legend of ShortSleeve Stan became the lore of Stan-and-Maria: a love story stitched together with stubbornness, laughter, a few tasteful pairs of trousers, and a city that knows a good compromise when it sees one.

THE DEVIL IN EAST AURORA

[Or How Old Nick Split His Lip]

An old New York folktale with only a little help from
Mason Winfield.

I

Most of us New Yorkers don't believe in the Devil any more, but it's not for the lack of commemoration. Between Chestertown and Warrensburg there's a deep gully the folk of Warren county call Devil's Kitchen. Near Elmira is a bend in the road so wicked they named it the Devil's Elbow, and the Devil's Nose is a Lake Ontario promontory. Near Rochester are two wet depressions, the Devil's Bath Tub in Mendon Ponds Park and the Devil's Punch Bowl in Mt. Hope Cemetery. The state even named a couple parks in his honor: Devil's Hole near Niagara Falls and one near Phoenicia called, too hopefully, I fear, the Devil's Tombstone.

There's a rumor Long Island was cleared of its stones by the Devil, throwing them all across the sound at the Native Americans who'd kicked him out of Connecticut. They weren't such good bargainers with the White man, tending to take him at face value in matters like that Manhattan deal; but the First Nations folk had had a good bit more time to get used to Old Nick, and him they knew how to handle. He can't go back to Connecticut, but he's still mad about it, and that's probably why he spends so much of his time in New York City, glaring across the sound.

They say the Devil's everywhere by now, and though his works are as prominent as ever, he seems to have kept himself pretty scarce around the south towns of Erie County in the last hundred years or so. But it's not like he's never been here. A story about 'Clootie,' as they sometimes call him, has been doing the rounds since the end of the 19th century.

A poor sculptor lived on one of the winding roads in the hills outside East Aurora. Jacob Hartmann was a big, powerful man who looked more like an old oarsman or boxer than the artist he was. Like a lot of people who never come to too much, he had great natural gifts. His statues, paintings, and sketches burst with fertility and power like those of the young Rodin. But in life, it seemed like he was always getting the worst of the deal.

Right out of school he had come to work at Roycroft, Elbert Hubbard's world-famous community of artists and craftsmen. Here too, something went wrong. They called the long-haired father of Roycroft a lot of things, but never a man who didn't know his own mind. Two like that could easily clash. But who knows? By the time he'd figured that Roycroft was not his ticket to eternity, the sculptor had a rickety farm house and a brood of children who never seemed to have enough.

The sculptor drifted into the Campus when he wanted work, so either his rift with Hubbard hadn't been too bad, or the great man didn't make much of it afterward. The sculptor may also have done some wrestling now and again with a demon they call rum, most often after the letters arrived from the ever-progressing friends of his academy days in Paris. The worst demon, though, was one he grappled with every day, his own paralyzing ambition, his failings in the light of the greatness against which he measured himself. He had a handful of his own natural demons, then, and no need to call in another. But they say before Nickie comes anyplace new, he has to have an invitation. Somebody asks him in, somehow.

There was a woman up on the sculptor's road, a big-boned gal called Massie MacLagan. Nobody knew how old she was, but her hair was still glorious and dark for a woman who'd been around that long. Everyone said she had magic of some sort, and a story was going round that she could call up the Devil when she chose. Some village lads said they'd seen her do it, and her neighbors all maintained that when their own cattle sickened, the milk from hers was sweet and abundant. Others scoffed though, that if she'd gone into business with Old Scratch, she wasn't a bargainer to be worried about, since she had precious little to show for it. But she had some reason for thinking well of herself, and one late July day she came by to see the sculptor's wife and was none too happy with her welcome.

The sculptor's barn came down in a storm that night, and the next day his neighbors helped him put it back up, hauling stones, timbers, nails, pitch, and tools from the Big Tree Road up the hilly track. The hot sun made this the heaviest work any of them had ever done.

That morning as the men worked, a beautiful black stallion was at the homestead, nuzzling and frisking with everyone like a puppy. No one knew who owned it. About noon the country father Augustus Murphy arrived on the scene to bless the undertaking and maybe inquire as well where certain members of the sculptor's family had been the Sunday last. He noticed the elegant stray horse and called some workers over for a word.

"Put a bridle on it, and work it as hard as you like," he said, "but don't give it any food or water. Mind me, now." And all the long day, the horse worked tirelessly, hauling prodigious loads of rock and timber up the steep road to the ridgetop. Each time they increased the burden, and each time the horse strained as it pulled, but it looked fresh as ever by the top. At last light, though, there were loads to go. As a final test they piled everything into several carts and tied them all together.

Horse and carts tore up the hill faster than the men could run alongside them, and they came to the sculptor's house to see the steed just dipping its head into a bucket that one of the neighbors, a lover of horses, had offered it. At its first sip, it perked its head up, gave a none-too-grateful look at the approaching workers, then shed bridle and harness and shot like an arrow into the fading woods.

The matter set tongues a-wag, and word of it toured town and Campus. The story was doubtless in its most developed form when the crusty handyman Anson Blackman–known to the world as "Ali Baba" through the writings of his world-famous boss–brought it into the office at the front of what became the bar of today's Roycroft Inn. It wasn't a total surprise.

Elbert Hubbard, "The Sage of East Aurora," had suspected that sooner or later the Devil would set his eye on the Roycroft enterprise and all the good work going on there. And Hubbard knew his former employee, struggling with, on the one side of his soul, the mighty aspirations only an artist can feel, standing in the halls of the ages, and on the other, the dreary failure he was to his children and wife. Success in either sense seemed to deny it in the other, and he may have seen no way out. In his rambles on the night-wild ridge, who knew what he may have breathed to himself or what he thought he wanted?

And it was just a bit later that summer that the sculptor was digging a well about the end of day. He looked up to see a stranger in riding clothes walking briskly across the field from the wood. He carried an axe, and led a goat on a tether. The sculptor didn't see how they'd made it so far into the open since last he'd looked. "Jacob Hartmann," the man said, his voice firm and clear. "You know pretty well who I am."

The sculptor didn't look up, but he didn't deny it, either.

"Here's a little something for you now. Why waste time, I always say? Time is money, I always say." The stranger chuckled to himself. There was something canny, even cruel, about his eyes. His teeth looked sharp.

"Now, you see this goat?" the stranger said. The goat's eyes looked right into those of Jacob Hartmann; it stuck its pink tongue out and bleated. Round its neck was a red and green ribbon, twisted into a sort of necklace.

"If you can cut off this goat's head, cleanly, with one stroke of the axe, you can be one of my greatest lieutenants. But if you fail at it, you'll be one of my lowliest servants. Now's the time. Time is money. What do you say?

The sculptor stood up shaking. He held the axe and the tether and took a good hard think.

Now, even under normal circumstances, the task was quite a bet. A goat is a skittish animal, quite likely to duck all over the which way, and a clean one-handed blow was pretty long odds. But the sculptor had swung many a mallet and felt in his heart certain he could do the job. He used a tree stump as a chopping block and stretched the animal's neck out across it, trying to hold it still with one hand. The goat looked up at him again as if it knew what he was thinking. That must have been what did it. The sculptor was a gentle soul for all his talk, and he'd never killed anything that had red blood in it. The axe fell from his hand.

"Hah! Just as I thought," snapped the stranger harshly. "When it comes to talk, you've a hearty heave-ho for any sort of a matter. When the chance is right in front of you and the means in your hand, you're not the man for it! Just as I thought." And with that, stranger, axe, and goat were up and away. The sculptor, sweating, wiped his brow, looked up, and they were gone.

The sculptor was filled with a lukewarm despair, as if he'd given away his only chance at amounting to something. But he wasn't completely sorry, as if he sensed that he had also avoided a terrible risk. In the coming weeks he was more at peace with his life than he had been before.

But the sculptor's oldest girl was becoming a woman early. She had a rough sort of beauty, a strong sensual body, a thatch of hay-colored curls, and sleepy eyes. She had, too, the touch for clay and chalk. One of her bright sketches had won the notice of the Roycroft painter Alex Fournier, and she had started to work and study with him. With all other Roycrofters, she was invited to the harvest dance in a barn of one of the Roycroft farms.

She was by herself for only an instant at the punch table when a stranger came up behind her. He smiled seductively, and before she knew it she was the belle of the night, with a dashing exotic gentleman devoted only to her, swirling her through every dance. His dress and his talk marked him a world traveler, surely some kind of aristocrat, surely one of the important people visiting Roycroft.

But near the end of the evening, who should enter the barn but Father Murphy, roused from his bed by some feeling that could not be denied. He'd saddled his horse, ridden to this very spot, and waited until he saw the stranger offering the sculptor's daughter a beautiful jeweled necklace, encouraging her to take off her own plain one with the cross on it. Hers was half over her head when the good father stepped up. Raising his crucifix, he blessed her and started chanting the rosary. With a curse, the stranger backed away; the girl shrieked and bent over, clutching the wrist the stranger had been holding. He had disappeared, apparently out the open window behind them. Marks like five fingers were burned into the skin of the girl's arm.

II

But that wasn't the end. A week later she took to her bed, the sculptor's daughter who had never been sick. She took a turn for the worse, and, as her oldest brother rode for Father Murphy, he saw a big black dog coming from the woods toward the house.

When the country father arrived at sunset the family told him a strange tale. The dog had found its way into the girl's room and they could not drive him from it. Father Murphy went in, and just after the door closed, terrible sounds came through it. The family rushed in and saw the good Father, his clothes torn, his face bruised, and three claw marks on his forehead. The dog was gone, but, if anything, the girl was weaker.

The Father had a strange tale of his own. He said that the beast had rushed him, beating him, clawing him, and throwing him around the room so he could not finish his prayer. It no longer looked like a normal dog, and it might have killed him. Then it perked its head up like it had heard something, and leaped out the window. He didn't know why it left, but the matter was too big for him, and he was going for help from a greater source.

Meanwhile, Elbert Hubbard was back in his hunting lodge on one of the woody hills of Aurora. This was a place a mile or so south of the village where the famous writer, publisher, philosopher and entrepreneur liked to get away once in a while. Sometimes it was for privacy. That night it was for some good private talking, with two of his artists, painter Alex Fournier and writer Richard le Gallienne–slender, goateed young men, inseparable friends often mistaken for each other. They'd all been to see the sculptor's family earlier in the day, but knew nothing of Father Murphy's visit or his adventure with the mysterious dog. They were well aware that the town was abuzz with supernatural gossip. The Devil had come to East Aurora.

The most recent version of the story had found its way to Hubbard through the ever-imaginative handyman Ali Baba. By then it included the marks of the bridle upon the cheeks of the young wasting girl due to Massie MacLagan's nightly ride of her through the Holland Hills. The three discussed the business well into their game of five card straight. Now, nothing rested on the play but preaching-rights and pennies; but bad loser 'Dicky' le Gallienne was losing badly, and irritably distracted by the talk. "The only Devil that I believe," he cried in his French accent, "is the one that can take whoever quits this game of cards!"

"That's the cider talking in you," said Alex Fournier, adding that they were tired and should all turn in. But le Gallienne wanted to get even, and shouted the same thing again.

"I wouldn't be saying that another time, now," said 'Brother' Elbert, the long-haired founder of Roycroft, in the tone he reserved for when he meant business. But le Gallienne was even madder, and said words to the same effect the third time. And on his echoes the door opened, and the country aristocrat from the Labor Day dance took an empty seat at the table. For a moment the only sound was the crackling of the fire. Hubbard looked evenly at the stranger, and his eyes gave nothing away. But those of Alex Fournier, who had been at the harvest dance, were white and wide, rolling to the side to look at the stranger without turning his face, for all the world like a vaudeville comedian impersonating a serving-boy frightened by a ghost.

"Might as well try a few hands," said Elbert Hubbard without looking up, knowing there was no other way out, and dealing in the Devil for a lark. And on the game went.

Hubbard was hoping that the candles or the fire would burn down in an hour or two and end the game with darkness, or that cockcrow would do the same with morning. But the fire strangely needed no more logs, the candles stayed tall and bright, and dawn was so late in coming that they lost all sense of time.

It could have been refreshing for Hubbard to meet the real Father of Artifice, since his own critics had called him that so many times before. And Nickie can be quite a talker when he has listeners who know something about history. He was about as happy with himself as he could be that night in Hubbard's cabin. The 1800s had been good for him, and he had such a damn good century coming up–the 20th, one he'd been planning since the days of the Roman Empire–that he was dying to tell somebody he could impress outside Heaven or Hell. He and Hubbard got into it pretty good, and except for the stakes of the moment, the time might have passed merrily.

As things went on, Hubbard was beginning to realize from the Devil's 'lean and hungry look' that he himself was the object of interest. The Prince of the Abyss would toss back any number of fledgling sinners for a single hook into a big one. Hubbard also knew that he would be bound to take whoever first put down his hand, and that Hubbard could save himself by merely letting one of the artists faint or nod off. Yet every time one of them drooped, Hubbard cut loose with an exclamation or guffaw, as if the Devil had just said the most remarkable or hilarious thing. Or he yawned, stretched out an arm, and tapped a shoulder, or kicked beneath the table. In each case the nodder stretched upright, cards in a deathly grip, as the moment and its impact returned.

There might have been a time when the grizzled handyman Ali Baba peeped in the window at his boss; and maybe again it was Father Murphy, battered but still game from his first losing bout. Both were later to say that the door had been held fast, and the cabin dim inside. But when the door opened, seemingly a night and a day later, who was it but Father Baker–Father Nelson Henry Baker of bridge and Basilica, Father Baker the someday-to-be saint, Father Baker the godliest man about the region?

"Morning to you, Father," said Elbert Hubbard, with a square glance and a slant of the brow. "Will you take a hand with us?"

"Sure as me faith, friend Bert," said the Father warmly. "I wouldn't pass up a good one." The Devil looked suddenly not so pleased with himself, but he didn't exactly object. The game set to again, but when the Father's turn came, he put his cards into his pocket with a smiling glare at the Devil. Old First Ward Irishman that he was, he looked at Old Nick like to say, You can try me, if you think you're the man for it.

The stranger sat there steaming. He knew he was licked, having been through something like this before with the Countess Cathleen, among others. So he just glared. The two artists nearly swooned, and it may be that even Hubbard himself didn't meet the gaze more than halfway. Then the stranger was up, around the table, and out the door so fast that no one could say he hadn't just vanished.

"Good on you, Father!" cried Elbert Hubbard, as Father Murphy and Ali Baba rushed in.

"You and your ideas have driven enough sinners back to the Church," said Father Baker. "I wouldn't miss a chance to do you a good turn back."

Alex Fournier quit wringing the holy Father's hand and Ali Baba stopped clapping him on the back only when someone noticed Dicky le Gallienne slumped to the floor. The painter fanned the fallen poet with a handkerchief as Father Murphy took his pulse and Ali Baba stood by criticizing. One of the artists later was to say he'd detected a whiff of brimstone when the stranger vanished; but the other was to ask him if he knew what brimstone smelled like; and besides, how could he smell anything passed out like he was on the floor?

Father Baker pulled Hubbard outside. It was late afternoon, which was all the more remarkable, since from within the cottage it had seemed dark as midnight outside. "I know you're not exactly of the faith," he said, handing Hubbard a medal on a cord, "but take ahold of this for just awhile. At sunset, as soon as I'm out of here, he'll come back to the sculptor's house. He may make a few requests, and no one must give in to anything, or the girl will be lost. It wouldn't be the worst idea if you hurried on out there. He'll be mighty persuasive, even for people who've been warned, and you might find a way to be helpful. He'll probably stick around till he gets somebody he wants, but least that young soul might be saved. Oh, and if you feel like taking a poke at Old Scratch, I advise against it," concluded the Father, shaking his head. "Keep to the letter of all the deals."

Just before sunset on the day with equal night, Hubbard waited in the sculptor's drafty home. The children and some neighbors were upstairs. The last bit of sun reddened the clouds above, three knocks sounded, and the beery voice of Massie MacLagan came through the door. "Sculptor Hartmann!"

The sculptor opened the door and stood beside his wife. There she was, Massie MacLagan, at the steps on a majestic black stallion that stood remarkably still. Little bits of leaf and twig were in its mane and coat, and it trained its eyes on them like no horse they had ever seen. "Give me her picture, and the girl is well," said Massie MacLagan, pointing inside the hall at the colorful chalk sketch, still with the ribbon on it, that had earned the girl her training at Roycroft. Nobody moved.

"Give me her cloak, and the girl is well," said Massie MacLagan, pointing to the hanger beneath the picture. This was the one article of value the girl had, a gift from an aunt in Canandaigua. Nobody moved.

"Give me her riding-crop, and the girl is well," said Massie MacLagan, pointing at some object beneath the cloak, knowing the girl's love of horses and thinking it her gift from the Jewett stables. Nobody moved, but at that instant Elbert Hubbard leaped from the closet beside the door with the big buggy-whip in one hand and Father Baker's amulet in the other.

"The whip it is, is it?" he cried, seizing the bridle of the mighty horse which, of course, was the Devil in disguise, and beginning to belabor him with the whip. Massie MacLagan, pitched at the first lick, lay off to the side rubbing her bruises, and fiddling with the bit of red and green ribbon twined about her neck.

Well, Hubbard lay into him for this and into him for that, at each blow crying out the name of some offended innocent or historic crime. He licked him for the Christian martyrs and the Spanish Inquisition, for the fall of Adam and the rise of Babel, for Torquemada and Cortez, for Simon Legree and John Brown, for the wars behind them and the drugs to come, for every time he could name that Ali Baba got drunk on payday, for every saint he had ever heard of and everybody he ever knew who had suffered some complaint due the Devil... and as we know, they are many. With such a power of belaboring and saintly-naming going on, you would have thought the man would run out of strength in arm or lung before the shrieking of the horse—which had not been very horsy at the start and had quickly become something like the yowling of a cat—drove everyone crazy. But Hubbard was strong of hand, they say, and stronger still of wind and words if there were listeners, particularly captive.

It's doubtful that any bit or bridle he hadn't put on him himself would have ever had power over Nickie. This one also was held by a hand with a holy medal in it, blessed by a living saint besides. For once, there appeared to be no way out but for Old Scratch to stand and take his medicine. This went on so long that the Devil may have been praying himself, for the Archangel Michael to come down and finish him, Judgment Day be damned. But eventually even Hubbard was slowing down, mostly because he was running out of names, and it looked like he was ready to let the Devil go. But then a keen look came over his face, and he said,

"And I can't forget one from my old friend…"–and Hubbard reared back with a stroke for the ages, one that would have done Vulcan, blacksmith of the gods, proud–"…Father Baker!"

But that was a blow that would have done it for the Devil, that even the Heavenly powers dared not let fall, summoning the last trumpet before mankind had half the warning that was coming to it. As the words came out, the eyes of the Devil-horse rolled over and back in his head, and before the fell blow could land he gave the fearfullest wrench on the holy bridle, doing fearfuller damage to his jaw. He tore out of there with a shriek like none of them would hear again, leaving behind a bloody bit, a handful of human-style teeth, and a houseful of amazed spectators.

Well, that was it for the Devil in East Aurora, at least as long as Elbert Hubbard was around. Word has it once you best 'Auld Hoofie,' as they call him, he'll keep himself scarce thereafter.

As for the sculptor and his family, well, the founder of Roycroft took more interest in them after this, and was able to send regular work the sculptor's way. It took a bit of bending out of Hubbard, that was all. It wasn't his nature, but he wasn't averse to it once he understood things a little better. It's not the usual way of the world, either, to lean toward people who insist upon it. The sculptor was never able to tame that pride in himself so that he could meet the world halfway, which was too bad.

And he never forgot his dreams for himself, and he died with them undimmed since his youth. The years had merely made him stop believing in them. But he had become better accustomed to his neighbors, and put enough into his work so that his family could have a little more of what they wanted; and his grandchildren wept for him when he was gone.

But that was how the Devil split his lip, and he's kept himself out of things first-hand around here for about the last hundred years. Though you won't know him by the whip-scars in another century or so, he hasn't been able to undo the damage he and the holy bridle did to himself, and he still talks out the side of his head. That's how you know if someone has really seen the Devil or not; if they don't mention that about him in their story, they're just making it up to suit their own politics.

©2025 Mason Winfield

AND THEN THEY WERE GONE ...
by: Ken JP Stuczynski
"Where did you come from?"

Those four words seemed harmless when Sam questioned the stranger sitting next to her. If she was surprised, it was that she wasn't surprised at all and should have been. It was the last bus of the night, and she didn't remember anyone else being on the bus, let alone next to her. It felt like a rhetorical question, but part of her expected an answer.

What appeared to be a man her age, dressed casually, stared at her. She might have thought him handsome if she were into that sort of thing, but it was more a matter of his looking comfortable, non-threatening. He seemed to give this question more thought than it deserved until he turned his head to the window and gestured to a light in the sky.

"That one."

If she had gotten on the bus just a few minutes later, Sam would have already heard the reports. These lights appeared by the tens of thousands. They were like star-toppers on Christmas trees, but the size of aircraft carriers, hovering just below the ionosphere. What was happening to her was happening all around the globe.

In a field in Vietnam, another rice planter appeared. In a restaurant in Boise, a waitress they didn't remember hiring started setting tableware. A customer at a mall appeared out of nowhere and began browsing clothes racks as if it were a sacred ritual, but didn't buy anything. An extra outfielder appeared in the top of the seventh inning at a minor league game in Japan, but missed an obvious catch. The stories were endless.

It could be said that the way they arrived was presumptuous – to just start dwelling in our workplaces, public spaces, and homes. But the opposite may have been true, where our concepts of personal space and social order were utterly alien to them.

Over the next day, more than half a billion new people decided to insert themselves into the commonplace activities of our civilization. In the confusion, some were nearly assaulted, but found themselves pacified or even asleep as fast as they could act. Some seemed to vanish as quickly as they came. Many were initially detained, until individuals with special titles and clearances realized it was too high for their pay grade. And a surprising number of them were greeted and even welcomed as if they had just come from the next village over, or a distant relative whose presence provides an excuse to bring out the good china. People couldn't wrap their heads around what was going on, and that was probably for the best.

In Sam's case, it was a bus ride home. "I don't understand," she said hesitantly, glancing from the window to her fellow passenger. Subconsciously, she perceived these lights were slowly changing hues and seemed to be neither planes nor stars. But it felt like her thoughts were on hold, not confused but not processing either.

"Do I know you? I feel like I've seen you before. Maybe you just remind me of my little brother." She shocked herself again. She never discussed her family, not even with her family, despite the limited contact they had.

"I am just me, so yes, you know me if you want to."

"Is that a pickup line?"

The conversations in these situations usually went from disbelief to belief astonishingly fast. In Sam's case, she didn't let go of the pepper spray in her purse until she got off the bus. But when he followed her off the bus, a boldness overtook her. She didn't need to see the news reports. She knew not just that we were not alone, but for the first time in her life, she did not feel alone. So she did the unthinkable. She took him home.

Into the night, a conversation almost too bizarre to recall culminated in acceptance of an unbelievable truth. The harder questions began. "Why are you here?"

"We have to be somewhere."

She hoped the Q and A that followed would make more sense after a good night's sleep. And she hoped the talking heads would fill in the gaps, for however much they could be trusted. When a super-earth-sized planet was engulfed by the clouds of Jupiter weeks earlier, scientists thought it was a random collision from an extrasolar body. But big scientific discoveries rarely make headlines. When they discovered four new moons in stable orbits around the red-eyed planet, it was beyond the average journalist to use as more than filler between advertisements on page six.

These new people weren't shy to tell their own tale. The star system they had been a part of ceased to exist countless eons ago. They evolved on the moon of a large rocky planet, and then over thousands or millions of years, expanded their habitat to its three other moons, all between the size of our Luna and the Earth itself. It was explained to us that the size of their bodies adjusts easily to different gravities such that they are over seven feet tall on their smallest moon, and shrink to under five feet on Terra Firma.

The question on her mind when she woke up late the next morning was, "Why do you look human?" She never gave it much thought, but intuitively knew beings from other planets weren't just humanoids with weird masks and silver jumpsuits. She was right – biologically, we had nothing in common with them.

He apparently didn't sleep and had just finished stacking clean dishes. This acceptance of shelter but not sleep turned out not to be an individual incident, but a custom of being indoors at night. We must call it a custom because they didn't sleep in the ordinary sense. Like the hemispheres of dolphins' brains taking turns resting and rejuvenating, they experienced a three-phase equivalent for whatever nervous system they seemed to possess. This is why they had trouble with certain tasks at certain times in the cycle and not others.

She asked the question, this time out loud. "Why do you look human?"

"I don't. You just see me that way. We don't want to scare you, so we have decided to take on your appearance for a while."

"Show me." Sam wasn't sure she was ready for this.

He lowered his psycho-holographic projection, like a soap bubble popping in almost slow motion. She was neither repulsed nor shocked. It was just … strange. She couldn't find a description fitting, but one might have described them as silver plantains with six to eight limbs resembling driftwood. A plethora of slits near what we could have assumed is the top or front were sensory organs of various kinds. Mechanical accoutrements to their lower or hind limb sets enabled upright locomotion and added height.

But by default, they preferred to look human. Light was manipulated to take on a rough, human-like appearance, resembling a mostly translucent and featureless mannequin shell. As a person of our species drew closer to them, our own brains seemed compelled to fill in the details with a visage of a familiar but unknown human, along with clothing similar to our own.

Sam liked his human appearance and felt a sense of relief when he reinitialized the projection. It was uncomfortable, at least for a time, to look at another being so alien, both figuratively and literally.

But there was so much more to this than appearance. Culturally, we had nothing in common. They did not share our mindset or social assumptions about survival, competition, jealousy, or power that have defined our genetic line since the Australopithecines. The commonality that enabled us to relate was, for lack of a better word, spiritual. There was a sense of respect, a desire to actively live in peace and mutual support, and a genuine, altruistic curiosity.

And this manifested in individual relationships. Sam's routines and habits were disrupted, or at least didn't seem so inviolable as they were. It was a few days before she told anyone about her houseguest.

"I feel like I adopted a puppy." Sam wasn't sure if she was joking or concerned as she talked to Ryan on the phone. "I can't believe I'm letting him … it … them stay here. Will I get in trouble? Should I call the police?"

"You're asking the wrong person, girl." She hated it when he called her that. Sure, she was a girl colloquially, but she never felt like a girl. It was more than being a Tomboy. She simply didn't have an interest in anything related to the label. "Look, they are freaking everywhere," accenting the word so that Sam could practically see his exaggerated body language on the other end. He was so dramatic, but also could keep a calm head. "It's like the gates of the city have been stormed, but by teddy bears. Nothing is broken. No laser beams. No probing the asses of the masses." Yeah, he went there, she thought to herself. He always goes there when talking about UFOs.

She wondered if such talk would offend her new friend. Friend? Did she just say the word, even if it was only in her own mind? "Well, I'm keeping him." She instantly felt a pang of regret speaking of them like a lost pet. Her mind was spinning, not in freefall, but more like a wobbly pinwheel with just barely too much wind to rotate without shaking a bit.

After a few weeks, it seemed official that all humanity was keeping their houseguests. No politician or ruler was eager to proffer what to do, or not do. We just didn't know what to make out of it all. Governments convened endlessly, with a blessed side effect that all conflicts essentially were paused.

But for all the confusion, there was no chaos. They brought about a calming effect in them. The belligerent or dangerously fearful among our species took on a pall of varying degrees of uneasiness, while the rest of us took on varying degrees of contentment and even happiness.

It's hard to explain the feeling itself. It's not like a drug. There is no sense of loss of will. It did not instill meekness or obedience, but rather receptiveness to the notion that things were going to be okay. For once, our fight-or-flight reflexes were overcome by reason instead of the other way around. We felt as reassured as we allowed ourselves to be, and even the histrionic and catastrophizing personalities among us seemed willing to loosen their ties and girdles.

Some of us – not in close enough proximity to feel the calming effect – were stirred up in a frenzy of concern. News outlets printed every possible opinion and conspiracy theory, no matter how unfounded.

Preachers took widely differing stances. Some chose outright denial; a few appealed toward thoughtful questioning; some reiterated claims to our god-given place of superiority over all creatures, even these clearly more evolved beings. They were implored as angels, decried as demons, proselytized to as heathen, or hailed as missionaries of a cosmic faith. They had no interest in our religion as anything more than another human activity. When pressed, at best, they refused to deny the legitimacy of any concept of deity except to speak of the "unnamable" in an almost personal way. Or perhaps we read into their words our own prejudices.

After all, they didn't speak human language. Their vocalizations were like wind instruments without reeds mixed with thumps, that is to say, resonant hollow tones beneath seemingly random tympanic patterns. But their technology approximated a word here and there in various languages, and like their appearance, our minds filled in the spaces so we "heard" a conveyance of thought based on our individual verbal skills and cultural idioms. This meant that digital recordings of their speech are mostly incomprehensible, just as video recordings show them as almost featureless humanoids with a hint of their true form, like a shadow beneath.

"What's your name?" Sam interrupted herself, "It feels like you've been here forever, and I can't believe I don't even know your name! What is wrong with me?" Since they met, it was all like a continuous dream, waking up a little at a time.

"We identify ourselves with certain sound patterns that your body can't naturally reproduce."

"What should I call you then?"

"Lee." She looked at him, then at a painting she did in art class, boldly titled "Bruce Lee – Legend and Dragon". It took up most of the wall behind her, serving as a backdrop to her entire living space. She let out an uncontrollable guffaw. It was another reaction that surprised her. Part of her consciously knew he looked a little like the martial arts superstar, at least in her mind. She had already discovered he had learned how to read, and he must have noticed how she reverently glanced at the poster whenever entering the room, like a kung fu mezuzah.

Their conversations were always about personal, everyday things. That was a bit of an achievement given all the fantastical occurrences over the next few months. The first thing on other people's minds was electricity.

The power grids of the developed nations started to fluctuate uncontrollably, but harmlessly. At some point, technicians discovered that shutting down entire plants – coal, nuclear, hydroelectric, or any other kind – had no effect. The power was still flowing through the lines, persisting in output at substations. But it was more than that. Devices powered by batteries no longer require recharging. A mild inconvenience arose, as some machines and devices had to be unplugged or modified with additional switches to be turned off.

For Sam and Lee, the conversation was on the ethics of whether or not to pay the electric bill. They never argued, although Sam occasionally became upset or frustrated. But she wasn't ashamed to be so … human. She had never felt so unapologetically herself.

"I don't know why I trust you." For a few days now, she has found herself thinking out loud. She had never done that before in her life, and now it was becoming a habit – or more like a release. "And I don't know why you would trust me. Nobody should trust me.

"Why not?" That would be the expected question, but it wasn't asked that way. It wasn't accusatory or confrontational. Her own irritable tenor was met with an almost impossible-to-believe innocence.

"Because … because … " Her voice trailed off into sobbing. With hesitation and stealth, he moved close; she felt his arms around her. She didn't care that there were four of them. He didn't have the warmth of a human being, but wasn't cold in any negative sense. It was like the refreshing coolness of the other side of the pillow when you don't want to be hot.

Her vision was blurred by tears … or was it being half-engulfed in a hologram? Through squinting eyes, she could make out his smooth, reflective skin with curious features, and there was nothing alien about it, just comfort. She hadn't felt that in a long time and didn't want to spoil the moment by overthinking anything.

Other people did think too much, though. Laws and agencies for reporting the location and activities of extraterrestrials eventually came into existence. Sam was supposed to declare her friend's occupancy and give a regular report on travel and behavior. Some who had such living companions made a desultory effort. Still, most people, like her, just didn't bother and the administrative officers didn't seem eager to push the issue.

Collectively, we agreed it made no sense to antagonize an obviously more advanced species. If not out of fear, it made good business sense to reap the rewards of planetary cohabitation. They lent us tools for unlimited power generation and gave us hints toward advances in physics and medicine, or more accurately, showed us how foolish we were in our distinctions between the sciences. There are still no words for the areas of study we did not imagine existed, and it is uncertain whether advancement in these new sciences is possible without them.

It was perhaps the first case in the history of our species where some "others" without tangible power were not regulated collectively into a lower class of personhood – or denied it altogether – by at least some state or principality. Mankind learned to play nice in this one significant instance.

Arguably, this detente was due to uncertainty, but it could also be attributed, in no small part, to human curiosity, whether for some benefit or its own sake. There were so many things to learn, both great and small. And we learn as individuals first.

"Come with me, Sam."

It was just a walk in the rain, but something about it felt like a life-changing proposal. Without words, she put on her boots and grabbed her umbrella. There was never a silence so loud. It quickly became a downpour, yet the absence of words felt like a sacred vow, waiting earnestly for a divine voice to fill the sky.

Lee kept pushing away the umbrella. He was always gentle, but this time it also seemed firm, with resolute intention. Never letting anyone get so close, she had never felt rejected before. But that is what she was feeling. As soon as the thought hit her, Lee stopped in his tracks, as if lightning had struck her, and he felt it through the handle of the umbrella they were both now holding. He pulled it from her now meek hands and let it fall unceremoniously to the ground as if it had merely slipped and was no longer there.

Her eyes slowly lifted, and what looked like a hand touched her face like she was the most fragile thing in the world. Valued. Cherished. She knew it was not rejection at all. She grasped the limb and pressed her lips to it with a pressure that unambiguously communicated a desire to never let go. The rain quickened its pace and ran down her like a waterfall, as if the cathartic release of a lifetime of tears.

Many of us were blessed with such a baptism, it seems, though perhaps not as personal. No one has ever seen them swim or go in water, but it was typical to see one stop whatever they were doing to greet the clouds as the first drops fell. After a while, it was not just the children who followed the habit. Mankind learned to love the rain. Even bosses started condoning "rain breaks" as a way to refresh workers toward more productivity.

Between huge benefits and simple lessons, we let our guard down. Over the seasons that followed, everyday people of the world came to realize there was nothing we needed to do. There was no problem to solve. We only needed to ask questions, listen, and do whatever seemed right. No desire for a torrent of pitchforks was ever realized.

They didn't take anything away from us – they only added. We are still unsure how they sustained themselves in terms of food and drink. There were reports of periodic raiding of landfills for various materials and possibly nourishment – cleaning up after themselves, of course – and we still are uncertain what was being removed. If it weren't for this, we would have assumed they had no needs at all.

Regardless, they were not oblivious to our own needs. They enjoyed helping farmers bring in unusually large crops, and many became employed in other necessary occupations, at least insofar as they worked and didn't mind not getting paid. This was a most difficult situation for companies and unions to navigate.

They didn't typically pose any restrictions on access to their ships in the atmosphere. But such tours were usually impromptu. An individual scientist or two had no problem being afforded a visit. Still, it was not often granted to bureaucratic requests of agencies.

"Do you want me to show you?" Lee asked Sam, as if it were a trivial offering.

"Oh, heck-yeah." It never occurred to her to ask, but she developed the habit of not turning down new experiences after meeting Lee.

In a blink, she was in a craft in the sky. Its innards were like a labyrinth or lattice of components and structures in all directions. It seemed there was gravity, but much less than what we are used to. There were no floors or ceilings per se – navigating was done by brachiating instead of walking or even climbing in the usual sense. The beings on board popped on their projections when they saw Sam out of respect for human prejudices, but they weren't necessary for her. She made a joke about already knowing what they look like naked.

"Are all the ships like this?"

"The shape and layout are the same, but the artwork and design are very different."

She didn't notice at first, but many of the components seemed ornamental, and she wondered what distinguished 'form following function' from pure whimsy.

"Can I see the Earth from here?" She didn't see any windows.

"Move to your left and hold onto that handle."

"Whoa!" The moment she grasped it, she could see the Earth below. But it was in her mind. She could still see everything around her on the ship. It was as if she were watching two channels at once and could focus on either one at will.

"I think I had enough fun for today."

Without ceremony, she blinked back, falling to her sofa. She could have sworn she heard Lee laugh, possibly for the first time.

There was no official distinction between human beings and those of other species in terms of everyday activity. The way they arrived saw to that. But some places were off-limits to them, as generous as they were with theirs. Between their technology and physiology, metal detectors blared, and even the most trusting guard tended to comply with the restrictions imposed by his superiors. Sometimes, escorts were assigned, a custom perplexing but accepted by our guests.

It took over four months for the unfounded fear of space-cooties to subside enough for visitors at health facilities to be welcome in some parts of the world. Appearing as nurses, doctors, or janitors, they went about their business as if they had always been there. They were difficult to work with. Their understanding of medicine made no sense. And neither did ours to them. Attempts at Q&A were usually short-lived, and each species consulted among themselves most of the time.

They rarely physically touched patients, but talked to them constantly. The exception was talking pulses and listening to heartbeats -- it was a human ritual they performed on everyone, whether they needed it or not, even the staff. They did touch instruments and machines, but more often appeared to stare at any given device for a long time and then walk away without comment. Rarely did they do anything to them that anyone could discern, other than what they were instructed to do by the official staff when they were accepted as part of the team.

Disturbing things would happen in the few instances they were allowed to participate in surgery. They would spend more time exploring than working, at least to our eyes. Somehow, they would cause the patient to wake up, anesthesia be damned, but they would be in no pain. In fact, a strange effect of joy would come across their face, often with tears, as they talked to the "doctor" poking at their insides.

It was another two or three months before the hospitals began to empty. A litany of ailments in ward after ward just went away. People with conditions based on genetic or cellular issues would have unexplainable changes in their symptoms and eventually have none, as if they'd never been sick.

The subject came up between Lee and Sam in a roundabout way.

"I usually get my allergies much worse this time of year. Did you change the weather?"

"That's not a good idea. We don't fully understand your ecosystem yet. But I saw your body having a reaction and adjusted the climate controls in the apartment."

"People are saying you're curing sick people around the world."

"I haven't been around the world, only this area, with you."

After so many similar conversations, it dawned on her once again that she was falling into the human tendency to think of a person as a group, or vice versa, through mere conversation. "Sorry, I keep doing that." Her words stretched out in more careful measurement. "Human people around the world are being cured, and they think it is because your species … people … are curing them."

"Maybe. Like your … species," Lee was weighing the words in similar fashion now, "we can figure out how an organism works and make changes to make them work better for the organism. If we can help, we do."

And help they did. All "treated" were later discovered to have lost all allergic reactions and have become immune to many of the effects of aging. In places where red tape was thicker than common sense, these benefits only occurred outside of the institutions from which they were barred. But wherever the newcomers were lodged, statistics of serious illnesses and medical fatalities dipped.

If the rumors were true, humanity was being lifted to a new plane of mortality, or even immortality. But the only image in Sam's mind was her grandmother. If these people had arrived sooner, could she have been saved?

After finishing some desultory tidying, her thoughts went back to Lee's attention to her needs and comfort, something he casually but unfailingly fulfilled. But gratefulness wasn't the direction her ponderings were pointed. She hesitated so many times to go down a certain path, but it was like the kettle had boiled and the lid couldn't stay on any longer. She finally breached the big question, though it came out like several at once. "Why did you choose to come home with me? Why do you stay here? What is so special about me? Why are you so nice to me, or are you just nice?"

The flurry of words was understood by her companion.

"There are many circumstances that brought us together." Sam's heart lifted a little at the acknowledgement that there was an 'us'. "I have met you and many others in my time here. I am nice." Sam was still put off by an honesty that was neither boastful nor self-abasing. "It only makes sense to me to do what needs to be done, both for myself and all around me, creatures and beings and resources." These dispassionate platitudes were starting to chill her hopes. "But it also makes sense to me that I will be closer to some more than others. I must choose to focus on certain beings, or even a single being more than others, to best live my life and do the most good."

The warmth trickled back, but the uncertainty yielded a further inquisition.

"Do you love me?" She didn't give any time to answer. "Because all those people who were supposed to love me didn't. I was a baby, then a child, now this–I don't know what this is." Even without an almost psychic intuition, Lee didn't need to prod. She told him about her childhood, a tale even an omniscient narrator would avoid repeating. "So if you are just being nice to me because you fell from the sky or whatever, and we're just friends and I pay rent and you do dishes, and–"

"Yes." She didn't remember Lee ever interrupting her.

"Wha–"

"I love you."

"But I-"

"You are just you." The phrase was familiar, but she couldn't place it. "There are so many things I learn from you that I would not learn or appreciate from anyone else. What you give me is yourself, and not anyone else. Circumstance is how we met, but I do not choose to remain here because of circumstance. You have chosen to know that I am just me and no one else. If others are capable, that is fine, but I do not need any other reason. I choose for you to be closest to me and have joy that you do the same."

There is no other way to describe the projection on his face and its correct interpretation by her psyche. It was love. Not the love of a boy fumbling to unhook a bra to become a man, or the love of a camp counselor so proud of how they can 'fix' kids, even if they are not broken. She had known those. No, it was most like the smile on her grandmother's face, hoping she would live long enough to spend one more holiday with the child everyone else ignored.

And as if sealing it with a kiss, more potent than he could ever physically express, he repeated those four most blessed words.

"You are just you."

We all clearly got the better end of the relationship while it lasted.

However, we did reciprocate in ways we did not at first realize. Our greatest machines were toys to them. Our technological marvels may as well have been sideshows at a fairground circus. However, they were fascinated by our arts, both in the performing and visual arts. They didn't care for radio or television except when they wanted to study something in particular. They were more interested in the specific–the saxophonist in the subway station, graffiti on an abandoned building, the hood ornament of an automobile. From their point of view, it was silly to enclose art in a building for its own sake. For the most part, they would rather visit a kindergarten and stare at the walls covered in construction paper and crayon marks. And they loved to dance. They couldn't really dance, mind you, but it never stopped them.

"You always laugh when I dance."

"I'm not making fun of you. It's just … so … unusual, Lee."

"My body and assistives aren't made to dance like human people."

"And that's why it's so endearing," Sam said, putting her arms around him. She got him to wear sweaters to minimize a reminder that he had extra limbs in his midsection. This made her wonder if she was a bad person. She wasn't prone to being superficial. But then she wasn't prone to being happy, either. She could no longer remember a time she didn't smile, but it was only half a year ago that she couldn't remember what smiling felt like.

Without vices and prejudices, anyone could find comfort in befriending. And there was no drama due to gender. Some people may perceive a particular being as feminine, while others may perceive it as masculine. Still, we soon came to understand that they could be male or female (in the strict sense of genetic contribution and gestation) at any given time, and were neither most of the time. In pairings of their own species, two beings may impregnate each other and both carry an offspring. Still, apparently, this is quite complicated when done naturally. Regardless, they were said to love as deeply as any human, always coupled with a general affection for all beings without distinction or jealousy. And while bodies and cultures couldn't mesh, they were still soulmates in so many ways to many of us.

"So … how is your boyfriend?"

Kim was making fun of her. She always made fun of her, but she came with the package of being Ryan's friend. Now that she had thought about it, it was the first time they were having lunch, just the two of them. The ulterior motive surfaced when Sam didn't retort.

"Ryan and I are worried about you." Still no response. "The people who care about you are concerned you're becoming fixated on that th- " An intruding waiter pouring water saved her from finishing her bigoted thought. "Person. Lee … mind if I call him Lee? I know Lee is a person to you and does the dishes and doesn't hurt you and all that …" The train of transparent insincerity would not be derailed. "But how does this work? How can you have a normal life?"

The last indictment was also the last straw. "Stop." The color of her face alone froze Kim in her tracks.

All her life, she was pressed like a piece of chewed gum between the pavement of what she wanted and the heel of social expectations. She was never allowed to be who she truly was. The words to describe what was in her soul weren't taught in school. They simply weren't in the public lexicon. And they were forbidden at home.

"I have never worn my heart on my sleeve, but I am tired of it being stuck in my throat. I don't owe you any explanation. You aren't my friend." She raised a hand to ensure she was not interrupted by dishonest contradictions. "But I am going to have this conversation rationally so you and other people will understand."

Kim slumped against the back of her chair, arms folded, but with the air of someone who knows they lost an argument and needed to take it with grace.

"Everyone talks about the spell they have over us. But I know the secret. I know how they do it." Her audience of one didn't know where this is headed and played the statue. "They-" she quickly adjusted her words, "Lee and the other people like him, from those moons, accept others. They listen. They share without fear. They ask without demanding. They help just because they can and won't hurt a fly to save their life. They are everything WE should be. They are what a friend should be, not like you."

Kim scoffed like a child at the playground. "Then why don't you just marry him!" Her eyes widened and bulged as the silence brought the realization. "Oh, Come on! Can you even have sex with that … thing?" All pretense at politeness was cast to the wind. "Are you going to have little green babies?"

Sam was nowhere as upset as either of them thought she should be. She felt impenetrable, invulnerable in her truth. Her voice was as even as water sitting in a glass. "What you are asking me is if I love him. YES. Would I marry him if there is a way? YES. Would I have children with him? YES."

"But how the h-"

"You and your sister are adopted, right?"

"But that's a wh-"

"And your parents are mixed … not that that concept has any meaning anymore to me. They are different religions and come from countries where people live totally differently from the way they do here."

Arms still crossed, she makes a final jab, the words drooling with sarcasm. "So love will find a way."

"Damn right it will."

Kim thought she knew her boyfriend's friend. They grew up together, at least as much as she couldn't keep Sam out of her circle of acquaintances. Sam was always the wallpaper, never the flower. She was supposed to be Dulcinea, not Quixote. She believed in nothing because no one believed in her. But now, things were unmistakably different. Shoving her highly fashionable hat to her head, Kim sprouted from her chair like a weed on steroids, and before bolting away from an uneaten sandwich, she yelled, "WHO ARE YOU?"

Sam's unbreakable smile proved she, for once in her life, knew the answer. And the mountaintops would listen if she shouted at them. But she didn't need to say it above a whisper, not caring she was the only one to hear it. "I am just me."

What many fail to realize is that each of us could have seemed like insects to each of them – or worse – and yet every move on their part, however misunderstood, seemed to be borne of genuine friendship. There was no intonation of dominance in their words; their actions spoke volumes of equality. But not everyone agreed. Some said their efforts to look like us and communicate telepathically were tantamount to deception and mind control. And yet there was no air of superiority to any of it. We were not enslaved. We did not become pets. And they took no advantage of "our" planet or its resources in any way we can tell. And despite numerous crimes against them, we seemed to be seen as a disappointment at most, like someone finding out their best friend has been talking behind our back and stealing money from them.

Just after the anniversary of their arrival, Lee sat down with Sam and turned on the television. It was to be a closed session at the United Nations earlier that day. Still, apparently Lee and others like him felt all of humanity had a right to know. It wasn't that they didn't grasp human notions of leadership or chain of command – they simply did not acknowledge them. To everyone's surprise, it was broadcast worldwide on every device capable of receiving audio or video for the next 72 hours.

A single viewing made it clear to all that the immigrants from the four moons sought an audience to address concerns, not a global forum to announce plans for world domination. The concerns they were to address were their own. They had a list of 2,013 questions, which the Earthling powers-that-be requested be narrowed down to ten questions, to explore them further in future sessions.

The first question, translated and transcribed by humans placed within reach of their psycholinguistic influence, set the tone.

"What is the necessity of borders?"

"We are many nations," the Secretary-General replied.

"That is not our question, nor an answer to it. Your maps show countless conceptual lines across the world, both great and small. We know that some collective bodies exist to administer services to various areas and not others. However, the borders we speak of do not appear to be functional. Many of us have been prevented from traveling from one place to another, even to see each other. This caused us to discover that there is strict control over your own people crossing these lines. It appears people are hindered from moving or living where they will, or associating with whom they will."

The Secretary-General began to speak, but his mouth snapped shut, and he fell back against his chair, befuddled. The visiting speaker had been chosen by the consensus of his species to speak because of his apparent expertise in human linguistics. An average conversation would be much simpler, but in psychically communicated elegance, the de facto diplomat continued, heard by each in their own language.

"You have an adequate ability to communicate and work together. You share a strong genetic and social similarity everywhere on this planet. We do not detect any possible biological threat to justify hundreds of large quarantined populations."

The representative of a small nation rose and shouted, "Not all of us can live with the rest of us!"

Immediately, another jumped to his feet and countered, "It takes two to make peace! We have every right to defend ourselves!"

The gavel put an end to the impromptu quarrel, and after the settling drone of angry muttering, the guest continued. "I don't understand. We do not find large numbers of your people wishing to harm each other, anywhere. Some are unsettled by losing access to lands in which they used to dwell. Many are hurt by individuals in everyday occurrences. Even more are hurt or taken away by individuals who claim it is their duty, or some administrative body of people represented here, compels them to do so. The vast majority of your species we have met do not have a nature or intent that is consistent with treating large numbers of people as separate from one another under any pretense of peace."

"That is a question for the philosophers," someone muttered under their breath a bit too close to the microphone.

"Who are these philosophers among you, then, that they may answer?"

"Certainly not here!" chided the representative from Greece, followed by muted chuckles across the chamber, but rendering only a puzzled, or perhaps disappointed look on the being at the center of attention.

"Let me make this clear," the next sentence started, at which point you could hear a pin drop, "I come before you not because you represent the people of this planet. You do not. You do not even seem to know or acknowledge that there are several other species, including people, also living on this planet. No, I come here because you represent highly limited numbers of people who have the ability to determine the fate of all the rest."

Trying to get back on track, the raised hand of a superpower's representative is recognized. "We have borders to protect the safety and resources of the people who live in a place so that the weak will not overcome the strong."

"I am aware that in many places there are police and laws that ensure that individuals and the things they consider theirs can be protected. This is not what I mean. I will try to explain another way."

The new tack continues after a pause long enough to make the recorders think something was wrong. "Your species is descended from creatures that formed separate groups for the benefit of selective breeding and keeping resources available to their group, excluding others. Violence was a trait carried in with other survival traits, including social traits intertwined with … tribalism … territorialism. You are now beings, and have been so for over a million solar years. You are no longer bound by your biology, but you have a choice. Even more, with knowledge and plenty, there is little reason to carry on such traditions even if your instincts linger on. But there is every reason not to burden yourselves. Why have you chosen this?"

It was like a cold shower had poured over the room. An aid began to visibly cry, and a few more pretended not to. A representative of another superpower was not immune to the calming effect, but by sheer effort was able to muster a frown of contempt and slowly rise to his feet. As his height increased, so did the volume of his voice.

"Have you come here to judge us?"

His unyielding glare was tempered, if not by the effect, by the look of pity on what was supposed of the speaker's face.

"We do not judge, not at all in the way you accuse. We discern. We are concerned for our safety as well as yours. I do not mean in the everyday foibles of interactions with individuals and their passions. We accept that in our time here, eight hundred eighty-nine of our people are no longer living because of the preventable accidents and the actions of individuals."

Another was about to speak, but quickly silenced themselves when the words continued. "We cannot hold this against you as a species, though such a way of thinking is common among yours. However, in addition to millions of humans in captivity, thirty-nine of our people are being held against their will in facilities maintained by the groups that claim authority over some of these border areas. A few are no longer living. We also know this is not the first time this has happened here to such visitors."

It was classified, but always suspected, that some of them were stealthily captured for interrogation, experimentation, and possibly dissection. But before anyone could raise questions as to what "not the first time" meant, the speaker concluded, "The heart of our questions is if we will become subject to the same tendencies and hindrances you have imposed on yourselves."

The glaring man, still standing, mustered his ire again. "We will not be judged! You came to our planet. We decide how we want to live."

The returned voice was almost soothingly gentle, but its content was an admonishment. "But you as a species do not decide how to live. A few of you decide how all shall live, even those not of your species. And to maintain this arrangement, you have so many lines that separate so many lives that would choose to be connected."

This brought up another point the speaker felt compelled to address.

"This is not one of my ten chosen questions, but why do you think it is your planet? Is it your moon? Is the Sun your star? When we speak of the moons whose journey we may command, it is not as if they are ours. They are not obligated to us. We have no claim over them that supersedes the claims of another. They are simply available to us and associated with us, like an ancestor. We may say someone is our ancestor, but we as descendants do not own them. You do not own your planet, or even your languages, styles of clothing, or shelter. You share them. You use them."

Hesitant nodding began but was quickly quenched. "But that is not what you mean by such words. You think we are invaders to take the place you live in because that is what you do. We cannot take what isn't yours, and we will not try to take what cannot be ours. Either we find mutual benefit, or we do not. There is no need for us to harm anyone, and there is no reason for you to harm each other or us. But we must not do nothing. A decision must be made, if not between us then among ourselves."

Those last words seemed to echo forever, and many were unsure whether it was the architecture or the psychoacoustic force that caused it. Eventually, a raised hand was acknowledged, followed by a dramatic pause of a delegate composing himself and adjusting his tie.

"Are you threatening us?" he said calmly. Jaws dropped, and eyes rolled. People shouted over each other, but his voice prevailed with the command of the active mic. "Because we know you aliens," stressing the word like an epithet, "have fooled our eyes and ears and influenced our thoughts since you came here. With promises of unlimited energy and resources, our own people don't see the point in paying taxes anymore. People aren't going to work. People aren't going to church, thinking you're all Jesus Christ or Mohammed come back from the sky. We are becoming weak and passive while you are just rearing to take over once we accept this space utopia we didn't ask for."

The calming effect was suddenly muted, which especially surprised the irate among them. The psycho-hologram was lowered, and the being from the four moons shone in its curved, reflective skin.

It wasn't clear to Sam what she was seeing at the edges of the television's screen. There was a lot of shuffling about the room. It looked like a few ambassadors lunged forward toward their previously welcome guest, while others blocked and restrained them. As much as those who deeply felt the truth in the visitor's communication sued for voluntary calm, it was confusion and fear that seemed to keep rash actions from taking over at large.

"We've got nukes!" one of the restrained delegates managed to spit out in earshot of everyone. No translation was necessary by the staff.

The psychoacoustics were still active. "I see then I must end this early with the last of our ten questions."

It was not calm that prevailed, but an awesome, terrifying curiosity. The Secretary General meekly nodded to the podium before him. From unknown orifices now visible surfaced sounds that the recorders rendered the following words in over a hundred languages:

"Why have you not heeded the warnings?"

Everyone looked at each other except those nations that possessed nuclear weapons, who simply stared, unblinking, at what they supposed were eyes.

The facilities across the world where these weapons are kept have been regularly visited many times since they were first invented. Their systems were powered down and returned to your control while the crafts affecting these systems were left visible above them during these instances. You cannot say you did not understand that you must reconsider what you are doing. The continued possession of these active weapons is a determining factor in how you are discerned as a species by all others."

Damning his prohibitions to confirm or deny such things, the man with the most stars on his shoulders said plainly, "That was you?" He corrected himself to be clear and polite, "That was done by members of your race?

"No, this is our first time here."

"Then … who are they? There's another race out there we need to know about?"

"There are many … races … who have visited to make nominal contact for such purposes." All could tell the word 'race' didn't seem right for the speaker.

"Well, if they're so far away we don't know about them, what do they care?" The military man had free rein of the floor, as the Secretary General, like most others, was composing themselves and trying to keep up, dumbfounded.

"You," beginning hesitantly, "are in a very crowded … neighborhood. You do not know we exist because most of us do not want you to know we exist." It seemed odd to human ears, but fitting, that the word 'we' was being used broadly enough to include all other sentient beings, except us. "It was under a set of complex circumstances of our journey that brought our particular species to choose contact with yours."

Sensing incomprehension, the psychoacoustic voice continued. "Despite high thoughts and many noble achievements, you have continued a nature that includes characteristics that, in practice, threaten your own survival. Pairing this technological ability and lack of restraint or sense to not use it, with your growing reach into your star system and someday beyond, your … neighbors … are rightfully concerned."

Before anyone could surmise that as a threat, the speaker made a final point.

"There is nothing for us to fear for a long time, so there is no reason to speak of action regarding this. There is hope that someday soon you will reconcile your nature with choice, and the few will no longer determine the fate of the many. We hope you will learn to recognize and commune with other beings among the creatures of your own planet, both on land and in the water. And we hope you willingly release to us those who were taken who are still alive. But there is no punishment in our way of thinking. Whatever suffering or joy is in your future will be of your own design."

These words were barely finished before the silver visitor disappeared in a flash of light.

"Lee, what does this mean … for us?"

"The ships are leaving. The people of my species cannot freely stay here."

"You can't … stay?" Sam almost stuttered the world's like a child afraid of the dark being told the lights have to be turned off.

"We would have to live in hiding."

She held him tight, hands under his sweater. With closed eyes and face pressed hard to the approximation of a chest, time stood still. And then she asked, with similar childlike anxiety, "Can I leave with you?"

"That is possible as well."

Weeks later, a bulge in Jupiter seemed to give birth to the planet it has swallowed a year before, and it moved off the orbital plane of the star we think of as ours, taking four moons with it.

There is no solid proof of any staying behind. The few among us – or perhaps more than a few – that formed marriage-like bonds were reported missing along with their celestial spouses.

For the rest of us, it was like an awkward breakup on a cosmic scale. There was no shouting match, no slamming of doors. We just woke up one morning and found out they had left, taking all their things with them. On the outside, it was like they had never visited our world. But even though they were with us only a year, the hole they left in our hearts and minds now seems like a vast canyon. Like falling in love, the average human being felt deep down they were always meant to be here with us, as alien as they were, literally and figuratively.

And then they were gone.

Like many a breakup, the lonely one finds the need to express their heartache. Art and stories inspired by their temporary presence, unavoidably rife with human prejudices and limitations, do not adequately describe those four bright seasons, nor the greyness that now follows.

Rain was never the same. Some said it was just psychic influence, but those who continued this ritual reported the psycho-emotional benefits as real, long after the exodus of our teachers. It would be nothing short of a blessing on the ages, if it were not another reminder of our loss.

Most bittersweet, their absence made us aware of something greater than all the technologies we may yet discover – that we were capable of sustained joy as a species. And as a species, we didn't deserve it, or them. We glimpsed the edges of creation with our telescopes and microscopes, but couldn't look far enough into others or ourselves to be worthy of not being alone in the universe..

The Horror of 1901

Austin Clark

At 4:07 PM on September 6, 1901, President William McKinley was shot twice in the abdomen by the anarchist Leon Czolgosz. One shot deflected off of McKinley's buttons; the other struck home. A rookie officer in the BPD, I was present when Detective Geary and the federal agent whose name I do not recall arrested the anarchist, and I remained part of the police detail that assisted with the protection of the President during his emergency surgery and subsequent palliation at John Milburn's mansion, where he had been staying.

When Vice President Roosevelt arrived at the Milburn House for the first time, I was surprised by two things: the intensity and anger in the man, and his aristocratic manner. The intensity was understandable, for this was the most serious business. The aristocracy caught me by surprise, as popular accounts depicted Roosevelt as an earthy man. I expected him to arrive in the attire of a soldier or the leathers of a mountain man, not well-dressed in a suit, waistcoat, and top hat.

His bearing was stiff as he brushed by to enter the room where the President was resting; he spoke not a word to us outside. When he emerged, his anger was quelled, and he himself was quite subdued; he lingered a bit to speak with some of the attending physicians and others outside; Mayor Diehl was present, as he had been with the President when he had been shot.

After talking quietly and somewhat harshly with the mayor and thoroughly interrogating the physicians present, I noticed that for a moment, Roosevelt had dropped his considerable guard; he looked gray and tired. I ventured to approach him.

"Mister Vice-President." I greeted him. "Sir."

He looked up at me, firmly in the eye. "Officer." He had been the police commissioner in New York, I knew. He was comfortable with policemen. He offered me his hand, and I shook it; his grip was exceptionally strong.

I had heard that the vice president was a Mason; as I had become one not too long ago, I shook his hand in a certain way. His eyes lit up, and he visibly relaxed.

"I thought maybe you'd like a cup of coffee." I ventured. At that, his expression brightened slightly.

"Officer, I've been longing for one ever since I stepped off the train. Please fetch one for me, and one for yourself. If they give you difficulty, tell them I insisted you join me." A chagrinned look crossed his face. "I forgot my manners. What's your name, officer?"

"Weschler." I replied. "Officer Timothy Weschler. How do you take your coffee, sir?"

"Half coffee, half milk." The vice president replied to me. "And today, enough sugar to stand the spoon in."

I hurried off to fetch the coffee; I took mine the same way. When I returned, Roosevelt took his cup and inhaled the steam from it gratefully, before he took a mouthful of it. The taste of the coffee seemed to further lift his spirits.

"Weschler. German?" He asked me.

"My parents are," I replied to him, "But I was born here."

He let out an approving noise. Then his thoughts wandered. "The doctors are optimistic, so I will force myself to be also." His expression was just that: forced.

I ventured to speak the truth to him. "…Sir, I haven't heard of many men who recovered easily from being shot in the gut, if at all."

Roosevelt let out a slow breath and looked me in the eye again. "Nor I, young man. In the army, a wound like that was a death sentence." He sipped his coffee again. "But I'll keep telling myself that William is strong; he will recover. The alternative is dreadful."

I could see what we both knew written on the Vice President's face; McKinley was sixty years old and fat, and the shadow of the angel of death would have been over us all even if he had been younger and stronger.

"Yes, sir." That was all I could venture. We drank our coffee in silence.

When Roosevelt finished his cup, I took it from him, and he shook my hand again. "Thank you for the reprieve, officer. I've got much business to attend to, and I hope to keep my time in Buffalo short."

I straightened up. "Sir."

He nodded, once. "As you were." Then he left me to attend to the rest of his business.

For a time, McKinley seemed to be rallying, and everyone was filled with an optimistic hope, myself included. I was assigned to the security detail at the Milburn House, where the President was resting, and as he seemed to rally, the mood was good.

Things began to take a turn for the worse the night that I saw the shadow while making my rounds around the perimeter of the mansion grounds. The night was overcast and dark, as nights in September in Buffalo so often are.

I was in the back of the house when something moved out of the corner of my eye, lurching in the manner of a drunk man. I raised my kerosene lantern and called out in a loud voice, "Who's there!?"

The light briefly caught the outline of a human figure, hunkered down and squat; as soon as the light touched it, it slunk away into the dark. I chased it, lantern lifted toward the back of the property, but found nothing, not even footprints. Everything around me seemed oppressive and strangely muted; the wind through the trees was bitter, even for September. When I turned to return to my post, I caught a pair of rats at the edge of the light of my lantern; they scattered, and I shuddered.

When I told the sergeant attached to our detail about what had occurred, he squeezed my shoulder. "You're just tired, Tim. You're on high alert and you're exhausted, and a thousand guys would tell you that's when you start hallucinating. Your shift's just about up as it is; go home and rest."

I did as I was told, but did not sleep well; I dreamed of that crawling shadow, and a carpet of rats.

Shortly thereafter, McKinley's health began to worsen. The optimistic mood everyone had been in dissolved, and was replaced with misery that turned into grim acceptance.

We were guarding a dead man.

The security detail was somber; we spoke little except as the work required it. I didn't seek the shadow again during my rounds, but I frequently saw rats scurrying across the property, which filled me with revulsion.

The President died at a quarter after two in the morning on September 14th.

Vice President Roosevelt returned to the city the next morning; I was not there to greet him. I was still on site at the Milburn House, as preparations were underway to embalm President McKinley and take his body back to Washington. He had been autopsied in the morning, not long after his death.

While I was standing guard at the back door, another officer came running up to me. "Tim!" He said, "The Vice President is here, and he's specifically asked for you!" He was impressed, and I was stunned with surprise.

When I attended on Vice President Roosevelt, he was alone in the house's parlor, and he had poured two cups of coffee. He looked gray, exhausted, and older than his years. "Tim." He looked up and then stood up to shake my hand. "Good to see you, man." He was finely and impeccably dressed, though he seemed subdued, and did not give off his usual outsize impression.

"Mister Vice President," I said, surprised at the informality of his greeting.

"Theodore." He said, gesturing for me to sit down. "We're on the level, now. You are Tim, and I am Theodore." He disliked the nickname 'Teddy,' I later learned; this was not a man who thought of himself in diminutives.

"I was discussing the past week with another officer, and he mentioned you had seen something on the grounds." He said as I picked up my coffee. He met my eyes, and his gaze was entirely serious. "Tell me."

I held my cup without tasting it. "Sir-"I began.

"Theodore." He said, irritation creeping into his voice. "Theodore, Tim, please. I need a tether to my humanity in this nightmare."

"…Theodore," I repeated. "When I was making the rounds on the night of the third, I thought I saw a human shadow, low to the ground. It sort of… slunk away from my lantern light, into the dark. The night was quite dark, and it was hard to see outside of the range of my lamplight. I shouted and followed it, but I didn't find anything there but rats; there were no footprints or anything else that indicated anything was there."

The President's expression tensed. "A shadow… and rats. Was the shadow hunched? Low to the ground, with arms that were too long? Like a chimpanzee might have?" He gripped his saucer, and I worried he might crack it. "Think, Tim! Think back. I need to know."

I thought back. "My view of it was just for a few seconds, s- Theodore. But…" I thought back. Its arms had been long; they seemed to drag near its knees, for all I could judge. "Yes, just so."

Roosevelt's mouth tightened. "And did you continue to see rats in a number that seemed out of sorts with the niceness of Milburn's house over the next few nights?"

I had! Every night on my patrol, I had caught a number of rats slinking away outside of the lamplight, and one of the cooks had shrieked in horror at finding a number of them in the kitchen about halfway through the week. I told him just that.

He sat back and was quiet for a moment. "I am going to go view William's body. I would like you to come with me; there is something I need to see." He set his coffee down, stood up, and offered me a hand to help me up. I gripped his hand, and he pulled me up easily.

"Have you ever seen or smelled the body of a man who's died of sepsis?" He asked me.

"I have, sir, mostly tramps." The bloat and the stink were revolting, and that was before they were opened up for autopsy.

Roosevelt nodded. "Good. That means you won't be taken aback. Let's go."

We ventured into the room, passing by the officer standing outside, and the smell hit us like a putrid wave; death and rot, so thick it felt like something we were pushing through to approach the corpse of the President. His body was lying under a white sheet, carefully draped, but there was nothing dignified about the bloated corpse underneath. One of the embalmers was there, preparing his instruments. He straightened up when we approached.

"Outside." Roosevelt fixed him with a look, and without a word, the man stepped away and scurried out of the room.

Roosevelt looked up at me, and then he reached back and carefully pulled back the sheet, folding it slowly as he went.

McKinley's body was horrid. Bloated and putrid, waxy and gray-green with death, his round belly mottled. The body hadn't yet been put back together after his autopsy; that would be the embalmer's job; he was still split open.

"William," Roosevelt said, at low breath. "He was not my favorite man, Tim. He was softness itself in his approach, though his mind was wily, and trying to make him see things my way was like punching a bag of sand. He yielded just enough to give me nothing. If he had been quarrelsome with me and fought me, I would have liked him better. And he thought little enough of me." His expression was somber. "But no man deserved this."

He began to go over the body, as if looking for something. He checked the neck first, and I heard him mumble, "…No, not here then; the clever leech would be more careful than to attach itself at the neck."

Finally, he looked up at me. "Tim, have you ever read Stoker's novel?"

"Dracula, sir?" I asked. "Everyone has read it over the past few years… It's thrilling. I had to limit myself to reading it on break during the day; doing so at night gave me bad dreams."

Roosevelt nodded once. "I met Stoker when I was running the police in New York. Oh, about seven years ago. Roughly two years before he published his novel. Stoker is quite Irish. As an Irishman, he was greatly interested in the welfare of the Irish in New York."

"We have a great many Irishmen here, as well, sir." I replied. "They dominate the south of the city."

Roosevelt grunted as he continued to check the corpse over, inspecting carefully. "I've often thought ill of them; the best of them stayed in Ireland and fought, and fight the British Crown still. They come from the stock of one of the most heroic and poetic races of mankind with a mythology as rich as that of the Greeks, but too often those I've met here have been ill-mannered, intemperate, stupid brutes. Many of the Irish policemen who served under me were wholly corrupt and immune to discipline."

I blinked, taken aback. Such sentiments weren't at all uncommon, but I hadn't expected to hear it from Roosevelt himself. "Theodore, I-"

Theodore frowned. "Unseemly thoughts, yes. There is a reason I say that, Tim. When Stoker visited New York, there was a rash of deaths among the New York Irish, all young women or children in the full bloom of health. Most ascribed it to the squalor in which the poor Irish live, especially in those days. But when I spoke to Stoker, he regaled me of the research he'd done and the accounts he'd taken as he worked on the story that would eventually become

Dracula." He had moved on to checking McKinley's armpits, now.

"As he spoke, the similarity to what was happening to those girls struck me like a thunderbolt, and out of a morbid sense of curiosity, I grabbed Stoker and pulled him out to investigate more closely. We visited the corpse of one of the Irish girls in the morgue, and I inspected the body, as I'm doing now. I'm no surgeon, but Stoker's accounts gave me an idea of what to look for."

I was terribly confused, but slowly the notion of what Roosevelt was saying began to dawn on me, and I was astonished. Was the Vice President looking for signs that McKinley had been attacked by a vampire? Had the stress of the situation caused him to go mad?

Roosevelt glanced up, and he could see the skepticism on my face; he ignored it and went on. "In the novel, the Count attacks his victims on the neck. This is sensationalist. As I checked the girl's body, the thought occurred to me that a parasite capable of thought and careful action wouldn't go for the throat; it's too obvious, too easy for someone to spot."

Finally, he moved down and began to inspect below McKinley's waist. "They would pick somewhere not easy to see, a place most men wouldn't look for propriety's sake, especially on a woman. Stoker and I finally found the injury high up on the inside of her thigh, near her groin-"He stopped, as he inspected the same spot. McKinley was very fat, and the mark would not have been easy to see upon casual inspection; in the discoloration of creeping sepsis and descent into death, it would've been harder still to find. But Roosevelt knew what he was seeking. "Look here." He gestured me in.

I put a handkerchief over my nose to block the smell and leaned in close. Indeed, on the inside of the President's thigh near the groin, there was what appeared to be an injury to the flesh, hidden among purpling, bruising, and the onset of decay. I knew the look of it; all policemen did. It was a human bitemark.

"Theodore," I said, and I endeavored to be very quiet. "This is all extremely unsettling. What you're telling me is fantasy. Vampires aren't real. But this-"I gestured. "There's no reason for that mark to be there."

Roosevelt looked up. "It is mad, isn't it? But I have learned one thing, Tim; even if something seems insane and irrational, you have to approach it rationally. The first thing you've got to do is accept that there are facts you don't know, and then act on the information you've got. When acting, the best thing to do in any situation is the right thing, the second best thing to do is the wrong thing, and the worst thing to do is nothing."

He straightened up and then carefully, respectfully folded the sheet back over McKinley's corpse. "There isn't enough time to regale you with the entire story of what Stoker and I found in Hell's Kitchen. I don't speak of what occurred to others because if I did, they would doubt my sanity, and probably rightfully so."

He stood up and held his hands up, prepared to decamp to find a place to wash them. "I don't know where it came from, Tim, and I don't know what spawned it, but Bram Stoker and I killed a vampire in New York City. And I am now convinced that a similar beast sped poor William to his death. Likely, he would have died anyway, but that's not my concern now."

He gestured for me to open the door so we could exit the room. "A creature like that – Stoker said that in Eastern Europe they call them strigoi or wampyr or nosferatu depending on where you are - will batten itself on the indigent, sick, and ailing; easy prey that can't resist. Then, as it gets stronger, it will go after sweeter prey. It cannot be allowed to go on as it is."

I cleared my throat. I was still dizzy from the notion of it. I thought it sounded rather pathetic coming out of my mouth when I finally managed, "Sir, you're to become president today."

Roosevelt looked up at me, and his eyes were afire. "Quite so. And as the President, the people of this country are in my charge. It is my responsibility to send this thing off to Hell before it kills again." Roosevelt was an avid hunter, I knew that. I got the distinct sense that he was acting out of both moral obligation and personal pleasure.

I will take the oath of office at three this afternoon. Tonight, I shall take you as my personal security detail, and we will hunt the hunter." He offered his hand again.

I stared at Roosevelt's hand, and then I shook it, slowly. "We're madmen in it together, then. I hope that this is a delusion, Theodore. I truly do hope so."

"If it is, you can personally escort me to that great brick barn of an Asylum and I'll submit myself to its care." Theodore replied, though the look on his face said he would do no such thing.

Theodore Roosevelt took the Oath of Office and became the President of the United States at 3:00 PM. I wasn't there; I was still on day shift guarding William McKinley's corpse as it was embalmed. He would then lie in state in the County Hall for the better part of a week before being moved to Washington. Roosevelt would be leaving the next day.

I waited for him outside the Milburn House that evening; it was still dark, and a chilly fog had risen; not at all uncommon weather. He adjusted his coat and opened it briefly to show me a pistol. I was similarly armed and carried my Kerosene lantern. It occurred to me that I was allowing the President of the United States to put his life in what might be mortal peril. He did not seem to overly care.

"I have told them that I need to find a place to have a drink and take a moment to gather my wits, and that I have picked you for my security. I'm famously good at getting my way on such matters." Roosevelt said. "But we mustn't tarry."

"I spotted the creature in the backyard. There were always policemen watching the mansion. I don't understand how it got in." I scratched my head.

"Through means I don't understand, these creatures move with rat-like stealth," Roosevelt said. "It observed, picked its moment – possibly when a patrolman was taking a leak in the bushes – and moved fast and quiet. And it got out the same way." He crossed his arms. "Like any predator, it expends as little energy as possible, so it will not have gone far. What else do we know?"

I thought for a moment. "…It dislikes the light, and its presence is marked by rats."

Roosevelt nodded emphatically. "Precisely, Tim. So it will be somewhere dark, and there will be an abundance of rats. We found the one in Hell's Kitchen in the sewer."

I shook my head. "Our sewers are mostly pipework, especially in these neighborhoods."

"Yes, and that in itself is an anomaly. These are creatures of filth and solitude, Tim. They attract vermin – rats, roaches, mosquitoes – and so they dwell in squalid places where they won't be noticed or where people generally won't go. But this is a grand neighborhood. So, where close by would this creature go that is dark, quiet, and where the things that proliferate around it wouldn't be noticed?"

A thought struck me. "…Forest Lawn is just a half-mile away to the north." The grandest cemetery in the city, huge and unvisited at night, a collection of nocturnal vermin would be unnoticed during the day, and a creature as stealthy as this strigoi would easily be able to sneak by the cemetery's groundskeepers. "But the grounds are huge."

"It's our best bet." Theodore said, before he turned and headed north along Delaware Avenue. "Come on, we'll need the light." I followed him quickly; he covered the distance fast.

When we reached the intersection of Delaware and Delevan, the spiked iron fence that bordered the cemetery grounds stretched ahead of us. Beyond, the failing light of the lantern illuminated tombstones and monuments in the dark. The fog further limited the reach of the lantern's light.

Roosevelt studied the iron spikes on top of the fence. "Nothing with a thought in its head would want to get torn up by those." He said. "Bring the light." He began to follow the fence. "The problem with grounds like this is that they are vast, and even regular inspections will sometimes miss things – here!" He gestured. "Bring the light closer." He pointed to a spot where the fence had been dug out underneath, as if by an animal, with loose dirt around it. A small and skinny man or a child would have been able to wiggle through it, just barely. "That's where it's getting through. Likely, the caretakers have already seen it and filled it in, and it simply dug the loose dirt back out. If we didn't know our prey, we'd simply call it a big groundhog or a fat skunk doing the digging."

I knelt down. "But how do we get in?"

Roosevelt shook his head. "We don't. The creature will be strong after having fed; as I said before, it'll be looking for something sweet to enjoy at its leisure. It'll take the path of least resistance and use the fog to our advantage."

I nodded, slowly, and then put out the lamp. We withdrew across the street and into the shadow of an old sycamore tree, and prepared to wait. As the fog grew thicker and chillier, I produced a flash from my coat pocket and offered it to Roosevelt.

"I don't partake." Roosevelt shook his head. "Fogs the mind, dulls the senses." But after a moment's consideration, he grabbed it. "Needs must when the Devil drives the coach," and took a short swig before passing it back. He grimaced. "Ugh! Brandy?"

"I thought perhaps it might be more to your liking." I said, before I took a pull of it myself.

"Ah. My secret's out. While most of the country thinks I'm of the common clay, you've noticed I'm posh." He said this slyly, as if poking fun at himself. "Everyone in New York knows I am."

"It would be hard to miss upon meeting you, sir." I replied, capping the flask. "I don't hold it against you."

"I've taken every possible step to avoid living a life of ease." Roosevelt replied quietly. "I've bad lungs. Always have. I remember when I was thirteen, the foolish doctors told my father I should smoke tobacco to "open up the lungs and allow air in." What nonsense. Anyone who's seen a soot smear up a wall knows that's quackery." He stroked his moustache with one hand and studied me through his glasses. "Fresh air and exercise are the best medicine for most things."

I had grown up a latchkey child in Black Rock, spending my evenings playing with friends until I finally had to slink home; what he said rang true enough to me. "Olmsted called parks the lungs of the city." I said, somewhat helplessly.

"So he did." Roosevelt nodded firmly. "And before long, science will bear him out." He glanced up and then narrowed his eyes and put his finger over his mouth. He gestured in the direction we had come. "Stay completely still. Don't move, or speak. Breathe shallowly and slowly."

At first, I didn't see anything, but between the two of us, I was not the hunter.

I heard it, before I saw it – the thin, reedy cry of an infant that had had half the life smothered out of it. My eyebrows rose, and I almost spoke, but then I remembered myself. The shape came lurching out of the fog. It was hunched over, one hand low to the ground; when it stopped to search, its palm was flat on the road. It cocked its head and looked about slowly, before it put its hand over the bundle in its other arm, muffling the infant's weak cries. Then it continued shuffling forward.

When it reached the dugout under the fence that we had filled in it stopped and let out a noise that sounded like a wet hiss of displeasure. With its one free hand, it crouched down to dig its access point back out. It scooped out handfuls of loose dirt until it had opened the way back up – then it unceremoniously pushed the infant through first, before it began to bend down.

This was when Roosevelt drew his revolver. He cocked the hammer back and fired – the creature lurched backward as the bullet struck its shoulder –

there was a dark spray of something into the air, and then the instant release of a foul, rotten odor.

Roosevelt stepped forward and fired again. This one struck it in the chest. This time, the thing in the dark stumbled backward, and then it turned and grabbed the iron fence. It vaulted it, and as it hit the spikes, there was a sickening, tearing sound. It hit the ground and lay limp like a corpse, but then it lurched to its feet, swept the infant up, and began to run.

Roosevelt cursed under his breath. "Damn the thing! I hit it square, too." He looked at the dugout and then at me. "I can't wriggle under there. You can. Go to it, son!"

I stared at it. If I had been a boy of fifteen again, I would've dared it fearlessly, but as a man of twenty-five, I was hit with the instant terror of becoming stuck, or of maiming myself. Then I thought of the child, and I dove under the dugout and began to wriggle through. There was a sharp pain along my back and the sound of tearing cloth; I silently hoped that my coat had taken the worst of it, and I forced my way through.

Roosevelt pushed the lantern after me. "Get after it!" He said. "I shall find a gate and catch up! Hurry, Tim! Hurry!"

I did not look back as I pulled the matches out of my pocket and re-lit the lantern. As I lifted it, I saw a trail of rotted black stuff. It had been grievously wounded by the bullets and the spikes on top of the fence! I sped after it, following the trail.

I tracked the creature's path through the headstones until I found its path to an old mausoleum, long fallen into genteel disrepair; the groundkeepers upkept it, but it was a place that had not been visited by family or friends in at least a decade, more likely two. Upon inspecting it, I found that the mausoleum's lock, long rusted and rotten, had been broken and carefully replaced; a gap in the door gave away where it had been forced.

I set the lamp down so that its light illuminated the door, found the gap, and pulled with all my might; with a moan of rusty iron, the door slowly gave way, and filled the interior chamber with light.

There, amid jumbled bones and a pair of smashed coffins, was a horror beyond all my reckoning. The light illuminated a creature, long-armed and filthy. It was naked, gaunt, and skeletal, its muscles withered tight over the bones, except for a bloated belly. Its lips pulled back from teeth that were sharp because they were broken, and the lantern light failed to penetrate the hollows where its eyes should be. The illumination revealed its shattered shoulder from Roosevelt's first shot, and the gut shot seeping vile dark stuff from the second.

A carpet of rats crawled around its ankles, making a hideous din.

I barely had time to think of the appropriateness of that before the thing wheeled on me and screamed, a hair-raising, frightful sound that would echo in every nightmare I had ever after. Rats poured out of the crypt and dispersed in every direction.

I swore and pulled my revolver out of my coat. I managed to shoot it once in the chest – I was aiming for its heart, but it didn't seem to care much – and then it was on me. It was ice-cold, and its grip was hard as steel. It snapped at me, biting into my shoulder but only getting a mouthful of my thick wool coat. It was stronger than me, but I had learned a thing or two wrestling larger, stronger boys in my youth, and I had leverage on it, for I was heavier. I lifted, turned, and pushed, and slammed its back on a nearby monument – there was a sick crack as it hit the granite, and then it pushed me backward off of it and onto the ground.

The lantern light illuminated it as it lurched its broken body toward me, mouth open – and then there was a shout and the retort of a pistol. The strigoi lurched backward from the bullet and turned to face Roosevelt, screaming again.

I scrambled to my feet and looked desperately around for my gun; it was nowhere to be seen. Roosevelt fired twice more, and his gun was empty. I heard him swear and then call out to the thing, "Come on, then! I'm ready for you!"

In a panic, I grabbed the nearest thing at hand: the kerosene lantern. I swung it at the creature's back, and there was the sound of shattering glass as the reservoir of fuel shattered and splashed over it, as the still burning wit lit the lot. The strigoi was wreathed in fire. It reared up, whirling and screaming that horrible scream.

I backed away, hurriedly, swearing loudly.

By now, Roosevelt had run in to grab the infant – he emerged holding the bundle, and grabbed my arm, pulling me away.

The thing flailed, and then it turned toward us. It could see us. It lurched forward, still burning, and then there was the crack of splintering bone. One of its knees had given out. It dragged its way toward us along the ground, one hand at a time, until finally its movements faltered, and it stopped and lay still.

My heart was thundering, and I took slow, deep breaths to try to steady it; the corpse of the strigoi was still burning fitfully. My lungs burned. I finally managed to gasp out, "Jesus wept!"

Roosevelt, while still visibly shaken, was altogether more composed. "Yes, that was visibly kin to the thing from Hell's Kitchen." He said. I looked at the bundle in his arm, and he shook his head, slowly, and gently set it down.

My stomach lurched. The failure to save the child must have been writ all over my face because Roosevelt approached me and looked down at the burning corpse. "That way likes madness, son. Think of the souls you've saved whose faces you'll never see. I'll have my men-"The President's men, "find the child's parents. They cannot be far."

I sat down on the nearest monument. "How do we explain this?" I asked. "Who would believe it?"

Roosevelt frowned, as if wrestling with something he hated. "We do not. We say nothing; an excuse will be invented, the story will go into the papers, and be buried by the sands of time. I detest lies, but I detest a panic that would lead to graves dug up and corpses mutilated more."

I shuddered at the thought and then looked at the thing, its hideous face turned slightly upward, and shuddered again. "And that?"

"I will quietly take it back to Washington with me; there I'll have some doctors that are worth a damn look at it and tell me what they can; I'll compel their silence, have the dirty thing incinerated, and once I've read the finished report I'll have it classified, sealed away and it'll be forgotten."

I glanced up at Roosevelt. "Is that what you did in Hell's Kitchen?" I asked him.

"No, in Hell's Kitchen, we destroyed the thing then and there and didn't tell anyone else." Roosevelt murmured. "Harder to cover this one up… but greater lies have been told before. By better men than us, even."

I thought about the thing, and why something so horrible was so secret; the only answer I could come up with was that I did not know and probably would never know, even though I detested it. I buried my head in my hands.

Roosevelt stood up. "On your feet, night watchman – your shift is done. Leave the remainder to me."

I nodded, slowly. As I rose, a line of Stoker's prose came into my mind, unbidden. I've thought on it often, since that night; I close this journal with it now.

How blessed are some people, whose lives have no fears, no dreads; to whom sleep is a blessing that comes nightly, and brings nothing but sweet dreams!

CRACKS MAKE YOU SPECIAL

Mark Donnelly, PhD

Nine-year-old Maggie lay curled on the living room couch, a thin quilt tucked to her chin even though it wasn't cold. The hum of the new refrigerator filled the quiet. Gleaming white, perfect, it had arrived last week. The old one–dented door, squeaky hinge–had stopped working. Her parents hadn't tried to fix it. They just replaced it.

Like Daddy's car after the crash. "It's totaled," he'd said, and they came home with something shiny and new. Better.

Maggie's fingers twisted the quilt. What if that's what happened when things broke? You replaced them. And she was broken.

She didn't tell anyone about the ache–not the one from chemo, but the whispering one that said maybe her parents wanted a daughter who wasn't sick, who didn't make them cry when she wasn't looking.

Did people wear out, too.

The Whispering Worry

At bedtime, Dad sat on her bed, careful not to squish Pumpkin the stuffed rabbit.

"How's my brave girl?" he asked, brushing her lavender cap.

"I'm okay," Maggie whispered.

Dad tilted his head. "Something's on your mind."

She hesitated, then blurted, "When your car broke, you got a new one. When the fridge broke, you got a new one. When I'm broken… will you get a new me?"

The room stilled. Dad's voice came low. "Sweetheart, you're not like a car or a fridge. You're our Maggie. There's only one of you in the universe. If the stars stopped shining, I'd still love them—but I could never replace them. And I could never replace you."

Her lip trembled. "What if I don't get better?"

Dad hugged her tight. "Then I'll love you just the same, forever. Nothing changes that."

The Star Jar

The next night, Dad brought home a glass jar. "We're starting a project."

"What is it?" Maggie asked.

"A star jar. We'll write down all the reasons you're special."

On colorful paper they wrote:

>I make the best blanket forts.

>Your laugh sounds like sunshine.

>You're braver than anyone I know.

They filled the jar until it rattled with stars. Dad held it up. "If this jar broke, I'd fix it. Because it's full of treasure. You're the same."

For the first time in weeks, Maggie's chest felt lighter.

Delaware Park

One morning she had energy. "How about the park?" Dad asked.

They packed a picnic and her rainbow-tailed kite. Maggie couldn't run like the other kids, but with Dad's help the kite soared high.

"It's like me," she whispered.

"Because you're flying?"

"Because the string is holding me up."

Dad kissed her forehead. "I'll always hold you up."

The Letter

That night Maggie wrote in her journal:

Dear Mom and Dad,

I'm sorry if I break sometimes. Please don't get a new kid when I'm too sick. I love you.

She slipped it under Dad's pillow.

In the morning, Dad sat on her bed with tears in his eyes. "Maggie, you never need to apologize for being sick. You're our heart. And hearts can't be replaced."

Hospital Nights

The hospital smelled sharp and clean. Maggie clutched Pumpkin as machines beeped softly.

Dad told her stories about building a failed go-kart. She giggled, then grew serious. "Did Grandma ever want to replace you when you got hurt?"

Dad shook his head. "I didn't love that car. But I love you. Even if you're sick, you're still Maggie–and that's perfect."

Mom added softly, "If I could sew up your worries and toss them out, I would. You're not broken. You're everything."

That night, Maggie fell asleep without the whispering worry.

A New Friend

At Roswell, Maggie met Ellie–freckled, red glasses, a laugh like a hiccup.

"Do you feel like a robot sometimes?" Ellie asked as they colored. "Like the tubes mean you're broken?"

Maggie's breath caught. "I thought maybe my parents would want a new kid."

Ellie gasped. "No way! My mom says I'm her favorite book. Even if some pages are wrinkly, she'd never throw it out."

Maggie smiled. "You can't replace a favorite story."

Before leaving, Ellie gave her a drawing of two stick girls under a rainbow.

On top: Not broken, just strong.

Maggie added it to her star jar.

The School Play

By autumn, Maggie was strong enough to visit school. Her class was rehearsing a winter play. She sat onstage with the others, nervous in her hat.

Her friend Jasmine whispered, "You look like a snow fairy."

When the play ended, the kids cheered for her. In the car home she told Mom, "They didn't see me as broken."

"Because you aren't," Mom said.

A Golden Day

One weekend, Dad took them to a pottery studio. On the shelves were bowls with cracks filled in with shimmering gold.

"This is Kintsugi," Dad said. "When something breaks, they repair it with gold, making it stronger and more beautiful."

Maggie traced the golden lines. "So the cracks make it special?"

"Exactly," Dad said. "That's you. Stronger, more beautiful because of what you've been through."

The Hard Question

After a rough treatment, Maggie whispered, "What if I don't get better?"

Dad's eyes glistened. "Then I'll love you every second. Nothing will take that away."

"Even if I'm… gone?"

He held her close. "Even then, you'll be with us–in stars, fireflies, and every piece of gold. You'll never be gone."

Somehow, the answer made her feel safe.

A Letter of Her Own

One bright morning Maggie wrote a note and tucked it into the star jar:

Dear Mom and Dad,

Thank you for not replacing me. You make me feel like I'm still me.

I love you bigger than all the stars in this jar.

Dad read it, smiling through tears. "Best letter I've ever gotten."

The Future Star

By summer, Maggie's treatments were less frequent. She still had bad days, but more good ones, too. One afternoon, as they added a final star to the jar, she said, "When I'm grown up, I want to help other kids who feel broken."

Dad hugged her. "You'll be amazing. You already are." That night, they sat on the porch. Maggie rested against Dad's chest, feeling safe and whole.

"Daddy," she murmured sleepily, "I'm not replaceable." "No, sweetheart," he whispered, kissing her hair. "You never were."

Confessions From A Hummingbird

by Avi Albert

There was a knock on our door. My mother, dressed the way she always did, in a coffee-stained nightgown, was in our tiny apartment's kitchen, scrubbing the dishes, when she heard them rapping on it. She was hesitant; she knew it was her no-good husband, he had been out since Sunday, three days ago. Whenever there was a knock, she'd glance at the calendar she kept on the cracked wall–marked up with the days he'd been gone, each X darker than the last. The nail holding the calendar seemed to be holding up the wall too; without it, she thought, the whole thing might've crumbled. It was like how it had always been since their separation. She tried ignoring these knocks–she really did–but there was something so obnoxiously obsessive about them, she couldn't bear it.

She threw down the dishes, which crashed into the sink, and stamped past me and Alvin, lying on the couch, listening to a static-filled baseball game on the radio. Alvin's got his red cap on, and his hand shoved way down in this baseball's mitt, I kinda… I kinda–okay, fine, I straight- up "borrowed" it for him. Don't wanna get myself busted. I mean it I'm really gonna give it back, as soon as Alvin outgrows the damn thing. He's hacking like crazy, but we're cracking jokes about those announcers, all metallic and robotic, like they're reading off a script or something–until, bam, there's a home run.

Alvin is six years younger than me–he's six–and he always dreams about being a baseball player. He'd want to be a catcher, and me a pitcher. But I couldn't pitch for shit, he damn well knew it too, after all the ball bruises he came home with. But he was always a good sport about it.

We used to play ball every day out in the backlot behind our tenement. We'd toss the ball, yelling out baseball players' names we imagined we were tossing at. Everything was going fine–during one of our longer pitching days, an exceptionally hot one at that. With what seemed to be a shortest possible time, he chased after the ball that whizzed over his head. In the next moment, he fell face down on the pavement, outstretching himself while reaching for the ball he couldn't grasp. A prized ambition now felled as his eyes wavered and the golden sights and sounds around him dimmed.

He was rushed to the hospital. I remember seeing him lifted into the ambulance, unconscious. I couldn't help but cry. He was only five at the time, just a year ago. I'd never seen anything like it before. I thought he was dead–and I thought I was the one who killed him. That's when they told us it was asthma. The real bad kind. The kind where even a powdered donut could trigger an attack. You know what they say? Follow your dreams? Well, in Alvin's case, following his dream of being a ball player would wind him up six feet under, and so he had to give it up. It was unfair he didn't deserve such crap luck, no kid did.

He should've been bitter. Hell, if anyone had a right to be pissed off at the world, it's him. Dad disappearing and reappearing like a magic trick nobody asked for, Mom barely hanging on, me being... well, me. Don't get me started, im a mess, really me, boy, I can't even stand me. Now that I think about it Kids are like flapjacks–the first one's always screwed up. That's me. And Alvin? Even though he's sick, hell, he's got a heart of an angel. Ain't fair, really. Is it wrong to feel somewhat jealous? He got the good heart and brains to boot, and I got... whatever junk in my noggin' is. I'm just all over the place, really I am, going mad like a rabid squirrel or something. Always burying my screwy sentiments like nuts. I don't know–maybe I'm just so sick of being cooped up, got no friends–just me and Alvin. But I guess that's all I really need, right? And yet through all the chaos, through his sickness, there he was–smiling like a dope, half the time, singing some ditty to try to cheer me up whenever I blew my top. I can never really remember how it goes because he always changed the lyrics midway through the song, he sang it as if it mattered, like it was the only thing keeping him from falling apart or something. I think it went kinda like this:

"The little birds fly high,

Watchin' the greens and blues go by. In summer breeze, they start off fresh,

Pickin' little berries for their little nest."

It was corny. Sweet, too, like everything he did, without realizing it mattered. It used to drive me nuts how fine he acted, still does. Like he wasn't carrying any of it. But that's the thing–I think he was carrying it, all of it, he just...carried it better. He didn't let any problem get to him, but it got to me, and bad, hell, a problem didn't even have to exist, and it'd still get to me. I'd invent 'em if I had to, just to feel something, anything. That's the thing–I don't know how to not worry. He kept it real he kept, all the shit seem like a joke. I always admired that about him. I still do. Not the smiling or the singing or the dumb stuff he said, but the way he refused to let the world make him miserable. He didn't fake being happy. He was the definition of happy, somehow, despite everything. And here I was, not being able to get through a regular Tuesday without feeling like I needed to bitch and moan. Even when things looked their worst, Alvin was right there beside me, keeping me from disappearing entirely. Hell, nothing was ever regular 'round here, it should be, but it isn't, I hate it.

I guess what I'm trying to say is—I was the older one, but he was the mature one. Always spreading some truth like the gospel, Just not in a loud, preachy obnoxious way that really pisses me off. He was our... no, my conscience, in a life that rejected any shred of decency—Alvin's the one kept the scales from tipping, and with it, all of us, like a house of cards. He had that gift, y'know? The gift to see golden horizons in the gloom and guide me there with him, only me— sorry, it's invite only—and I gotta admit it's nice... no, not nice. Paradise!

The door swung open, and in came a gust of cheap perfume and booze, foul as rot and just as thick. My father was leaning on the other side, about ready to topple over. His bleary face was smudged with either fresh slugs or tender smooches; we assumed it was both. My mom could only say, "Who was it this time, Bill?" as she would inevitably cast her gaze down as she asked almost subserviently. I hated her for that; there was no way in hell I would ever give my voice over like she did. Today was like any other day that he chose to grace us with his rot-n presence. As he was trying to stumble in, my mom suddenly grabbed a broom and began swatting him away, keeping him from entering. She knew damn well who he'd been with—she always knew, just from the perfume that clung to his ratty clothes. This time it was Nancy Sullivan, the lady, up on the sixth floor.

That's how Bill—my father—spent his days: going door to door, shuffling through the hallways in a drunken stupor that smelled like cat piss. There's this nutjob down the hall—she's got, like, a bazillion cats running wild all over the place. They piss and shit everywhere. Nobody's checked in on her in a long time, and now the cats are all over the hallway, clawing at her door, trying to get back in. But it's locked. And the smell coming from her apartment is godawful. I think she kicked the bucket. I swear she has. But no one bothers to do a damn thing about it. It makes me go crazy—thinking she's rotting in there, and everybody's curious, but nobody does a damn thing. People are afraid of him, and I don't blame them–everyone but the women, who'd gladly invite him in. Mostly, they were old curmudgeons, the crusty kind who are seeking the thrill they found when they were younger, much younger.

"Boys, go to your room!" she snapped, broom still gripped in her hand like she might swing again.

We clicked off the radio and shuffled off, me helping Alvin along–his breath wheezing, he was quaking in his pajamas. We got into our room, and I shut the battered door with a slam. The hinges have spent many years out of alignment, having never been repaired.

Our room was nothing more than a shell with peeling wallpaper, yellowed where the radiator hissed and banged all night long, keeping us awake and alert. At times, Alvin thought the sound was a monster, always startled by its insatiable clanking. Water stains that bloomed on the ceiling seemed to stare down at us, as we drifted off, barely, to sleep each night. I won't start about the worst nights of all. Summer it was, and summer it was when, judging by the alley screams, loud weepings, and constant fights. No one else seemed to sleep either, like a night long feature showing a potboiler bunch of cops, robbers, flatfoots, and victims. Late, late on darkly lit nights, I used to wonder as I started to doze, 'Did ma leave the radio on again?'

A single twin mattress lay on the floor, springs poking out, with wads of stuffing busting out of the torn mattress cover. An old milk crate served as a nightstand, stacked high with crumpled comics and empty matchbooks. Our crummy room was full of these bugs–cockroaches, bedbugs, or whatever–they always looked bigger than they really were. And they sure bit like hell. Every morning, we'd wake up riddled with marks, like we'd come down with the chickenpox overnight. But we didn't just see the bites as trouble. We turned them into something else–drawing tattoos on each other with whatever we had, pencils or crayons, tracing over them itchy bumps. Those janky tattoos were our way of making the worst fun, making 'em real sharp. I don't know, we didn't give a damn about how goofy we look, we had nothing better to do. I have a real killer shark doodled on my cheek that Alvin drew.

The air always smelled stagnant, reeking of some foul household odor and something sour that never quite settled, no matter how often mom opened the window. Just outside, on a crooked little branch, at odd times, a pesky robin, a pigeon, or a house sparrow might settle there, looking maybe suspiciously inside at all of us.

There was also a little bay window with a built-in bench. It touched a huge tree that had odd- shaped flowers we called city roses, or rose of the city, or some weird name. Hell, any name we spin up sure beat the craphole that stinks up its outskirts. Alvin and I would sit on that little bench. I taught him how to bet odds on card flips. Some pimply ash haired punk had taught me this trick while swiping all my cards at each toss…I lost Lou, Babe, Hank, even Willie. I would rather forget it all. Though playing with him in his huge purple jersey left an untrenchable memory. The ease with which he stripped my trusting deck bare, taught me something about how long even the best things never last.

That window faced the sunny side. There was a wall of bright green flecked with sunlight, which cast a mottled shadow upon the bench and oakwood floor. One morning, while we looked down after a card match, we saw it. A tiny shadow that flashed as it moved like a bolt, right through the dark and light pattern on the floor. It was creepy. "Did you see that?" "What?" I lied. "No.." I involuntarily gulped. 'These things happen,' I heard old Aunt Rosa say. I could not remember why. I looked up. Adjusting to a sea of green around us. The overwhelming view encircled us.

Spring had become a reality in our apartment. How had we missed it? We were within that field of green, punctuated by shards of light which quavered and expanded, glowing very brightly then subsiding. That was something, but the bolt caught me. A tiny green and red iridescent bullet. It did not veer off course; rather, it seemed to spin a trajectory at right angles, then almost haphazardly change direction. Then, most surprisingly, hover...in place. The pink, red, and white roses formed another layer to observe, placed within, around, and before the great green sea in front of us. Blue, red, pink, and white blossoms were also contained within a sea of golden sunlight. The brisk and purposeful pilot. A lone hummingbird became our quiet little friend after we took notice of him that day. In fact, there, at that little bench beneath the window bay. There on the old floor. That's where we ate lunches in summer and avoided assiduously in dark winter. There in that tiny space, we built a world. I took a Coke bottle and filled it with sugar water at Alvin's insistence, hoping we could see him dart by and enjoy the sweet water we set out daily. To others, it may have been a waste of time, but to us, it was the only thing that kept me sane. Its iridescent shine always seemed to lift our spirits in the many dismal hours spent in isolation. My mother spends hours frittering away on things seemingly futile, never brought to completion.

She did, however, always notice the bird and its shimmering glory and commented, "Oh, how pretty! Look how fast it zips–just shows up."

"Why don't you take a closer look?" I would say, but s

he would reply the same way she always did, "I've already seen it, dear, no need to go out now." We were well used to her nonchalant refusal to join us outside, as we could hear the door behind her after her frightening attempt outdoors and into the uncertainty of the world. No amount of reasoning could bring her out.I sat Alvin down on the mattress, and he leaned back, eyes dull and chest heaving as if catching his breath, he being winded as usual. He was hugging that old mitt of his–like he always does when things get bad. It's like whenever he holds it, every problem just disappears.. It's as if just dreamin' up baseball games, hearing the cracks of the bat, the roar of the crowd, just everything keeps him from croaking. And hell, he's got every damn right to dream it. Thing is, I don't want him just dreamin'. To me, dreamin's great and all, but truth is, it's just a waste of time. All that time spent dreamin' is less time doin' somethin'–anything. Why would you wanna be a vegetable, sittin' there shittin' yourself, waitin' on someone else to wipe it up? I want him to live it. Maybe that's me bein' selfish. Hell, maybe all we get is dreams–and not much else. 'Cause everything else? It's so damn expensive.

"You alright?" I asked, forcing myself to smile, a real goofy one too.

He nodded, barely, little liar, I could tell he wasn't. It was a stupid thing to ask, he was never alright when dad came bursting back into our lives. Neither one of us hated him for leaving; we didn't understand it but trust me when I say I despise him for returning, Alvin, not so much. He hardly knew the man.

I opened the door just enough to watch my parents' conversation. I listened attentively, though I couldn't make out every word. But I knew what it was– another one of those infamous handouts my father always seemed to beg for. The same desperate tune, a never-ending cycle.

"I need sixty," Bill blurted with a burp.

"You're gonna have to get it someplace else, Bill," she said. "C'mon, darling, I really need it this time. This is different."

"Different from what? I told you, and I'll tell you again! We are done, Bill, we've been done for a year. So stop coming 'round smelling like a brothel begging for handouts, I don't have anything for you! Why don't you ask Nancy Sullivan or Donna Haywood for something? Im sure you won't get anything! THAT'S WHY YOU COME TO ME …WHEN YOUR SPENDING FUN IS UP!" she screamed, red-faced.

"That's not true… I miss you and the boys. Don't think I can ever forget you. Is that fair to me?"

"What's fair? I have forgotten, and you keep coming back asking for more and more and more. I don't have anything. And remember our kids? I have to handle them, I can't look after you as well! Less you're a kid too, coming back at your whim, doing what you want in this building. All ears are in the hallway! Its damn embarrassing, Bill! Everyone knows what a louse you,-"

Before she could finish, there was a sound that made me shiver; it was a sharp, cruel blow, a streak of lightning flashed across my vision. I could hear the sobbing after the shocking slap. "Shut your filthy hole, Linda-"

Upon the sound, Alvin collapsed onto the ground with a loud thud, lying motionless. I didn't even consider his condition in that moment–before the slap. The shock must have triggered it. I rushed over to his side and tried waking him. His breath was shallow, his heartbeat fading fast, and he began to flush into a shade of purple. I called out to him, as I began shaking him, I screamed in his ears, pleaded to him to wake up–until I had no voice left to give.

My mother ran to me, saw me shaking Alvin's limp body, hoping for any kind of response. My dad paid no attention. He just stood there, in a stupor, warbling incomprehensibly, crying about the money he was owed. I didn't expect anything less from the man who ran from his family. I just wanted to kill him.

"Colt, get the inhaler! It's in the cupboard in the kitchen!" my mom shouted frantically, muttering under her breath, "My boy, my boy…"

I did what I was told and scrambled to the cupboard, my mind flashing emerald green. I climbed onto a chair and reached inside. In a desperate flurry, I flung the contents out in every direction.

"It's not here!" I shouted.

"Check the medicine cabinet–quickly!"

I ran through the cluttered mess, nearly falling over. I yanked the cabinet open and pulled out an inhaler, testing it–just a sputter of dead air. It was shot.

My face burned red with rage–rage at my mom for not replacing it, rage at my dad for setting all this in motion, and rage at myself for believing I could trust anyone to get anything done. I was hoping for a miracle.

A miracle? There's no such thing.

I bolted back with the useless inhaler. "There's nothing left in it!" I cried.

She snatched it from my trembling hand and crammed it into Alvin's mouth, pressing it over and over as if she somehow just believed hard enough, something might still come out.

"Come on–come on, baby! Oh God, please save my child," she whispered. She gasped as each click of the empty inhaler felt like a countdown.

I couldn't help but roll my eyes. With all the prayers and desperate bargains, you'd think God was running a racket–giving out raffle tickets with a million-to-one chance of winning. Far as I know, God never picks up requests, and sure as hell doesn't answer. Not around here anyway.

There was nothing, no sign of life within his body. Just silence. Just Alvin. We were both speechless, what more was there to say but cry as she cradled her baby boy's body, my hands clutching her shoulder, trying to comfort her, then she flicked her hopeless gaze to Bill.

"Bill, we need you. He needs you," she said, breath hitching. "The pharmacy–it's across town. His prescription it's under Alvin Knox. They'll know. Please, Bill."

"Oh, so now you need Bill, huh? I ain't runnin' errands for the likes of you." "But he's your child, Bill! Please–don't do it for me. Do it for Alvin."

"They're not my problem. You made sure of that when you kicked me out. They're your problem now."

"Please, Bill… have a heart. Just once. This is more important than anything." "If it's so damn important, you go and do it!"

He scoffed and seized her wrist, wrenching it, jerking her up to her feet. Her eyes snapped to the door, wide and glassy, like a deer spotting headlights. Her courage faltered as her feet were rooted to the floor; as if every thought of hers implored her not to go out, you could just read it on her face. To step into a world she didn't feel connected to, that she didn't want to be connected to, was worse than death to her.

"I-I- can't!" she stammered, brittle by the thought of stepping out.

"You can't? Or you won't?" Bill sneered as he twisted her wrist as if trying to break it. Bill dragged her through the apartment, ignoring her blubbering protest. I pursued them, begging my father to let her go, but he shoved me aside. Not wanting to be restrained any longer, my mother dug her fingernails into Bill's arm, leaving tiny puncture marks. Fed up with her retaliation, he slung her over his broad shoulder, but she kicked and erratically flailed, trying to escape Bill's hold as he neared the door. Bill yanked the door open and promptly dropped my mother on the threshold.

I heard my mom squeal–her little voice drowned out by my father's shouting–as she went on begging my father to let her back in. But he just laughed–same old Bill.

Before I could make any sense of what was happening, I rushed to the window and watched my father shoving my mother off the stoop with his beefy hand, a hand I wanted to bite off; hell, that hand never fed me anyway. The door slammed in her face. You'd think with all this blasted commotion, it would bring out people to help. But nah. You would be wrong. I shoulda figured nobody would ever stick to good morals and actually do something. I'm never surprised by folks around here and their big talk. It's all load of bullshit if you ask me. They're always running their mouths whenever there's a crowd to give them the attention they crave about helping people, like they're some kind of prophet. They actually believe their own crap, like just saying it makes it true. Like they don't have to do a damn thing–just spew shit–and that's supposed to fix everything. Believing their own garbage enough to get them into a good spot in heaven or wherever. It's all just shit… ever damn word of it. It really drives me bonkers.

I dared myself not to cry. I really did. But the tears just came, loud and stupid, and louder still. I banged on the window, crying to my mother. I tried to get to the door, but it was guarded by an ogre.

I whizzed off like a shot and charged at my father–all that was missing was the meep meep. I headbutted his fat belly, and the next thing I knew, I was clonked right on my ass. It sure hurt like hell, too. Just as I was starting to get up, he grabbed me by the collar and hurled me aside. I felt like a damn bowling ball barreling into the corner. After crashing into the wall, I crawled over to the window and kept watching her fall apart. I was still dazed, seeing a double of everything–like I couldn't stop the world from spinning. But as quickly as it came, it left me with a horrible sight: my trembling mother, consumed by fear and chaos that seemed to be devouring her whole. For cryin' out loud, she just stood there, as if her soul was sucked right outta her– Like some goon spun up a crazy idea and dared her to play freeze tag with the Grim Reaper, and she was dopey enough to listen and had the moronic moxie to go on ahead with it. I just didn't understand it. What was so frightening? I saw her cautiously turn around, trying to maintain some sort of composure, but every inch of her was quivering. She had no shred of grace and did a crappy job of faking it. Then I swear I saw what I saw, at least I think I did. She's mumbled about it for years. I could never get any answer out of her; she would just casually dismiss it, brushing it off as if it were nothing. Just a bad day, just a bad dream, just her "nerves." In a dizzying flash like from a camera strobed crackling through my vision–it's as if I'd gone blind just for a moment until my sight came back–a filthy mugger, warped and hysterical, he was there, gun and all. I couldn't wipe his ugly mug o' his away no matter how many times I shouted and shut my eyes, hoping he'd just vanish, but he didn't. The dizzying heights, the flood of trampling feet, the nameless strangers–all of it thundered around me. Too much. Too loud.

Too fast. The world wouldn't hold still. My brain just came apart, it all got scrambled y'know? Like you tune in on the radio and all you get a fuzzy gibberish crap. I couldn't help but hold my breath–the only way to survive that rambling chaos–even though I wasn't outside with her. I just needed something steady, anything, so I wouldn't pass out. I don't know if I actually saw him or any of it. Maybe I'm just as nuts as she is. Maybe none of it really happened, and I'm just making it all up to feel something… something… real.

But whatever it was, I couldn't shake it. I couldn't shake her. It's like she couldn't help it–like she was just another sucker caught in her own trap. She just couldn't help herself as she came bolting back inside like it was the only thing she could do–while Bill was too busy with his damn flask to care. Back through the door, back to Alvin, she dropped to the floor beside him and held him tight. She sobbed harder than I'd ever seen her, trying to drown out whatever the hell she saw. Real loud. Loud as those insane sirens I hear in the middle of the night.

"Their faces. The heat. The noise. I just wanted it to stop, all of it!" she cried. It was like everything she blurted out split her wide open, and her mind was collapsing right in front of us.

In the middle of my mother's pandemonium, shrieking in absolute horror, and I swear I heard the windows shatter, she was that loud, it's as if she just got staked right into the center of her heart, blood kept spurting like a geyser I saw in some magazines. She might as well have been staked. It would've been a blessing in disguise, if you wanna know the truth. All this crying and no damn fight in her, it really got to me, it's like she already gave up on her child. God its so damn ridiculous! I mean how she can go on blubbering without doing a damn thing, without trying, anything, anything at all? It's like she already checked out. I'd already slipped my Converse– fallen apart, taped just enough to keep 'em from fallin' apart–and whipped on my green windbreaker, all faded olive, figuring I could blend right on in with the city lousy liveliness with no one noticing. Real incognito, right? Like hell anyone'd give a damn to look twice–hell, even once is more than generous. It's beat to hell and stitched upon stitch. If there was one thing my mom was good at, it wasn't the meals or overall comfort. None of that sentimental crap–she was too caught up in her own grievances and fantasies of places she wished she'd traveled but got too old, crazy, and flat out broke to visit any of them. She'd sit zoned out, staring at those glossy travel magazines of Hawaii, Paris, or the Riviera. Those magazines only made her cry and whimper like those stray dogs out on the sidewalk in the rain–the same ones the so-called kind people kick just for being there. You know the kind: those phonies, always going on about saving the world? Like hell they do. They don't give a damn about anything but their own talk.

She'd go back to knitting, listening to some crappy soap opera she gets too damn emotional over, too wrapped in her own problems up to bear any of mine or Alvin's. No, it was patching up our torn-up clothing; she always wanted us to look our best and presentable. I don't got the darndest idea why–who was she trying to impress? 'Round here, if you're struttin' all spiffy like, you're just askin' for a boatload of trouble–like with a wad of moola dangling on your jacket. It's a rare sight and a lucky day for a bum to get all bold and plant you flat on your ass on the pavement, with nothing left but a bruised ego and a fat lip.

I went to my mother, who was still crying, and rested a hand on her back, hoping to somehow ease her pain, even just a little.

"Don't worry, Mom, I'll get Alvin's medicine. Just please stop crying."

I lunged for the purse on the kitchen table, digging through the clutter until I found five crumpled dollars and snagged a scrunched-up pack of Luckies. I stuffed the cash into my jeans, the smokes into my windbreaker. But the moment the cash flashed in my hand, my father shoved me aside and tore into the bag himself. He yanked out a hidden wad of bills, eyes gleaming, then bolted for the door. I sprang after him, but my mother's voice stopped me cold.

"Don't," she said. "Let him go. Just please hurry back. Take a sandwich with you."

"Won't be long!" I replied quickly, making a bologna sandwich between two moldy slices of bread, spreading the mustard, and placing it in the brown paper bag as I zipped out the door and onto the street.

I ran like my life depended on it–but his life actually did. Past cracked sidewalks and broken fences, each step echoing the thought: He could die. He could actually die.

It wasn't supposed to be like this. This wasn't supposed to fall on me. But it did. Because no one else would carry it. Not Mom, not Bill. Just me.

I bolted down the block, heart hammering, the sound of breaking glass chasing me. Neighbors leaned from windows, shouting over each other–rage, warning, or just noise, I couldn't tell. Bottles smashed around me like hail. Maybe it was random. Maybe it was for me. I didn't plan to stick around to find out.

The city boiled in concrete and chaos, a jungle without vines–just fire escapes and rows

of faded hopscotch boards scribbled across every vacant lot. Sure, there were gardens, green patches squeezed between busted buildings, all bombed out to shit, but nobody gave a rat's ass about 'em–overgrown and wild. The flowers and plants seemed to stretch high to the clouds. I cleared a way through the tall green stalks as I marched step by step through the dirt. Rows of giant ants marched beside me, carrying pieces of leaves and enormous scraps of people's lunches; they were all headed toward the ant hill. It stood large right before us, its peak touching the murky sky beyond. The city's smog seemed to be wavering through the rumbling hill itself as if it was about to erupt like a damn volcano. I booked it–like my ass was on fire–the second I heard those thudding feet. It was like a damn earthquake; I could hardly stay on my feet. And that's when I saw it–a massive shoe stomping down. The marching ants were toast– absolutely squashed flat. That was it for those poor bastards. Game over. They were turned into pancakes.

Antcakes. God, those feet were enormous. All that was missing was that crummy old Fe Fi Fo Fum garbage. Then came the buzzing. Bees. Bees! A whole swarm of 'em. The biggest stinkin' bees you ever saw, and they weren't happy, you can forget about that. They were chasing me, tryin' to jab 'em red-hot stingers at me. What a real mess I got myself into.

Finally, the bus stop appeared through the steam rising off the pavement. Relief. Sort of. The flaps of my aviator cap were slapping me on my cheeks as I ran harder. I kept the cap on 'cause it fit, and because of its rank, it smelled like shit. I found it in a dumpster beat to shit like a dog's chew toy, and people usually left me be, the way I wanted. The hat kept all their lousy noises away. This old cap of mine made me feel invisible and soar above the clouds. I always wanted to fly; I didn't want to be all cooped up. Hell, if I had one wish I wanted so desperately to come true was to be able to fly, I used to think about it all the time, what a waste of time. I still can't believe I bought into that bull. The thing about wishes is, they don't fix anything. If anything, you become sadder and sadder each damn day your wish doesn't come true, it's all just a big lie.

Wishes are so damn corny if you ask me. You only make one when you've got no other way out. And when it doesn't come true–and it never does–you feel like a bigger moron than before.

That's why I stopped wishing. Hell, I wished not to wish.

The bus stop was nearly deserted. Just an old woman hunched over on the bench, muttering to herself as words spilled out in fragments, something about seeing her grandson and how he was running late or whatnot. She was real doggone ugly too, she look like a hairless pitted ass of a mole rat, no foolin', Scouts honor! She was wearing that kind of clothing that would draw the most unwanted attention, jewels galore, I don't know if she was lost or something, in fact, I'd say this old crow came straight outta a coffin. No bus yet. My lungs burned. I let my legs give out and dropped beside her, breathing hard. She turned to me and gave me the creepiest look I've ever seen, like the kind of look that someone starin' right through you. "Oh, there you are, Henry! It's about time!" She turned to me with her foggy glasses, thick as hell–like the bottom of a bottle. I swear she looked at me like I was the last face she'd ever see. "Im sorry but I ain't Henry," I replied, trying to be polite but sounding like a damn moron. "Why, sure you are! Look at you–all grown up! You're the spitting image of your father, you poor devil!" She reached out with crooked fingers and pinched my cheeks–real hard too.

I never knew an old bat could be so damn strong, I felt as though she could tear my cheek right off, if she wanted to. God, what kind of meds was this dried-up hag on? And don't even ask about her smell, man, it packed a punch; she had that musty smell that it seems every old hack obtains God, it smelled like some old crusty sock left in a flooded basement. What's even worse is she knew she damn smelled like death too and tried to compensate with this intoxicating cloud of perfume she had spitz on, the real nasty kind too! The kind that could make you go blind just from the eye-watering whiff, like tear gas!

Then this guy came clacking down the sidewalk like it was a horse track–fancy duds, panic all over his clean-shaven face, without so much as a speck of dust on him. His shock white hair with jet-black streaks ran down his forehead like a real crappy dye job. "Mom! Mom, it's me–it's Paul. Let's go, okay?! Were you here all this damn time, we've been looking for you all morning!"

She looked at her son wiping off her glasses and back at me, confused. The smile dropped from her face. "But he was just–he was right here–"

Paul wrapped his coat around her shoulders. "Mom, Henry's been dead for seven years now! Why do you keep worrying us half to death with all this running around? There's no need to keep coming to different bus stops, he's gone."

"But he was right there, he was coming to pick me up!" she shouted, wagging her finger at the empty bus parking spot.

"Come on, Mom, let's go home. Rachel is waiting for you with some hot chocolate. Would you like some?" The son, his arm latching around her gently, prodded her to move along.

"But there he is now!" she said, gesturing right at me, trying to pull free from his grasp.

"No, it's not, Mom, he's just a kid! Henry would be twenty-five now, don't you remember his accident?"

She kept glancing at me over her shoulder as she was escorted away, like maybe I'd vanish if she blinked. And for a second, I felt like I had.

I was alone, sinking into the depths of the unknown, with no map to guide me, and I may never resurface again. Would anyone ever notice me missing? Maybe that's just what a lost boy is– someone who disappears, and the world keeps turning anyway, and only the lost will be replaced by someone else to fill their shoes with a new name, a new story; there are plenty of them to fill anyhow. It's like there's a row of pegs and when each coat is taken off, another one's hung up in its place.

I tugged a Luckie out from the pack with my mouth–like I'd done a thousand times before– more outta habit than anything. It's not like I like to smoke. It's just something to pass the time with, y'know? A comfort. And before I get the third degree from anyone–yeah, yeah, I've heard it all before. All that "smoking kills" propaganda. But I think it's all just a stinky load of bull. If it's not one thing you're hooked on, it's another. I do plan on quitting. Maybe. I don't know. Like, maybe someday–maybe when I'm old and baggy. But what's the point then? I would've made it that far. Why stop now? Even if I hack up a lung, I still got a spare. Am I wrong? But now that I really think about it, you know what they say about quitters–"winners never quit," or however it goes–and I'm never one to quit anything. So I probably won't.

I flicked out my Zippo and started doing tricks with it absentmindedly. The click of the lid was satisfying, and I kept lighting it, staring at the flame as I tested my courage by burning my thumb, feeling the heat bubble up under my skin. The pain was somehow entertaining–maybe I was just cracked–but I still got a strange kick out of watching the scorch marks form on my fingers. I lit the cig and took deep drags, just trying to distract myself from my gut-wrenching thoughts, trying to shake that whole scene off me.

The bus shrieked to a stop right in front of me. I didn't realize its arrival until the last bit of my smoke scorched on my finger, reeling me back to reality. I flicked the butt onto the side of the road and watched it roll into the sewer grate. Then, finishing my bologna sandwich in one humongous mouthful, I crumpled the brown bag and tossed it onto the street. With swift steps, I launched myself toward the bus door. As others scrambled off, I clambered in–only to be knocked back out by the rush of passengers piling out. Stumbling, I caught myself and hauled myself in.

I stood before the cross-eyed bus driver. God, it was creepy–I didn't know which eye to look at. One eye was darting one way while the other stared right through me. I felt like I was trapped in some weird staring contest, without a chance of winning. He was waiting for change. He didn't say a word–he didn't need to, his weary-ass face said it all. Like he knew he was the punchline of every damn joke about what kind of job you land when you don't you don't properly apply yourself–like how that hell were you suppose to do that, bring a nice juicy apple for teacher was gonna save your sorry ass? Nah, the way I see it, the deck has already been stacked against you from the moment you take your first breath. Every ounce of whatever dignity he had for himself was beat the shit outta him and whatever remained was slurped down by that nasty mug of coffee he was nursing, leaving nothing but an empty stare.

I locked eyes with him, and boy oh boy, he looked beat. From the slump of his shoulders to that dead, emotionless glare of that '…please, kill me…' plea. It struck me hard. I figured I'd wind up like him if I hung around here too long. Hell, who am I kidding? I'm the spitting image of this lump of lard already. I haven't got the faintest idea if I'll ever get out, even if I wanted to bum rides and go somewhere cold, somewhere desolate, hell like Antarctica or Alaska, anywhere cold will do, somewhere I can just hide in an igloo and freeze my ass off and go fishin' all the time, I can go ice skating anytime I want maybe I'll join one of 'em tribes of Eskimos and chow down on some of their famed ice cream pies–and I gotta say they're so damn good they are my favorite treat. Thing is, every time I get one of 'em pies from the ice-cream truck, it all melts into a goopy mess as soon as you rip it out from the wrapper. Now that I'm thinking about it, I'm too yellow to remotely go through with it. Oh God, let it not come true–the last thing I ever want is to be trapped in this shithole for the rest of my life. But knowing God and the way He is… hell, He probably has worse planned out for me.

"Would you quit staring and give me the change?!" the bus driver groaned and squeezed this giant, hairy mole on his chin. I swear, that was the only thing on him with hair–hell, you could cut it with a lawn mower. The more I stared at it, the bigger the mole seemed to grow!

"Right." My hands dug into the pocket where the money should've been– only to end up fingering through a tear in my pocket. The whole damn roll of bills was gone. I almost passed out, there was nothing but that damn hole. I didn't know what to do. Alvin depended on me. It seemed the whole world just froze, like for once the streets stopped honking, the birds stopped chirping, babies stopped crying, everything just… dead. It's a funny thing that the time you most need something, it never appears. I needed to get across town but had nothing to get me there with. That got on my nerves real bad.

"My change?!" the fat ass driver let out a hoarse grumble, getting real sore, as he tapped the change box, glaring at me like I'd just called his mother every dirty name in the book. I stood there, my face pale as a corpse–hell, I wished I were a corpse right now. The other passengers, all ticked off like him, started yelling at me. I don't know what they thought yelling would do– make me move faster? Gosh, I must've looked like a total sap just gawking there, my mouth hanging wide open like that. No, if anything, it made it worse. I just spiraled deeper. I couldn't concentrate on jackshit.

I had nothing. Nothing but the weight of saving Alvin, but even that seemed pointless. Hell, I couldn't even keep track of money–how could some poor schmuck like him count on me?

Hell, one time we had a goldfish, and I kept forgetting to feed it. It died in no more than four days. I remember just staring at that fish floating on top of the water, dead. I really didn't care about it. I felt the burden of taking care of it was gone, and honestly… I was relieved.

Hell, I don't know why any parent would give a kid a useless pet like a fish. You can't do anything with the damn thing–no tricks, no fun, just… nothing. As I think about it now, I feel like that dead goldfish, once swimming in its own filth, waiting for something. Then, poof–a couple of days after being left to yourself, you just die.

I swear, when I'm dead and gone, I don't wanna be missed. Hell, no one would give a damn. No, I don't want none of that funeral rites crap. Those are all corny. The people you hated the most show up and somehow convince the others how much you meant to them and all that other pretentious bull. I just want someone to flush me down the toilet, my feet sticking out of the toilet bowl, all crooked–just like we did with that stupid wide-eyed guppy. No big deal, no ceremony, no 'oh, how sad,' just gone. That's about all I'm good for. If you really wanna know how fleeting mortality is, just get a pet, any kind of pet will do, anything but a stupid pet rock that is. Nothing is more depressing than having fun with your pet, then it gets sick and you gotta put it down, and expecting to replace that same enjoyment with a new one? To me, the pet game's just a crummy goddamn racket all set up for the likes of needy suckers that want a cute companion to feel they're somehow fulfilled or whatever. A grab-and-go furry factory, all wrapped in a package with a ribbon on, with zero thought to the attachment or heartbreak involved. Have a friend for a couple of years, then expect to get a new one once it dies on you? Nah, I'll pass on that. I sniff a royal ripoff.

That's the part they always leave out. And I totally get it; it makes sense to me. Hell, the last thing anyone wants is a kid with their snot all bubbling out, busting their eyes out over it, and making a big scene.

"I don't have any." I whimpered, trying to hold out from bawling.

"You don't have any?"

I instantly dropped to the ground, burying my head in my forearms, hiding my face with my aviator cap. It was loud...really loud, and it hurt. I was somehow winded, something pushed the puff right out of me. Then, boy, did those tears I desperately tried to hold come bursting out. I hadn't cried–not since Alvin collapsed, that is. There never seemed to be a point in crying… until now. I didn't feel any tears until now. Now I let everything out, I couldn't stop blubbering, not if you even paid me to. It was embarrassing. I didn't care, though. I tried forcing myself to stop, but I just cried damn harder and louder.

"What the hell is wrong with you?" the bus driver barked, all set to toss me out to the curb. I didn't know how to respond, and I practically choked. What the hell isn't wrong with me, I found myself thinking. Not being able to go to school like normal kids, make friends, do all the crazy fun stuff kids are supposed to do before you grow up and you look stupid doin' it–sometimes I look at the playground, see all 'em kids play, man, do I wish I could just go over and swing to my heart's content–like normal boys should, live it up, before life ain't there to live it up to no more–but there I go, a wishin'–'cause I was caught in the trenches of the adult world, with damn bombs goin' off everywhere, shackled to goddamn meanderin' odd jobs–overworked and underpaid, bringing home mere pennies, barely enough to scrape by.

Nah. No school for me. I dropped out in the eighth grade. Had to.

After my old man bailed, someone had to step up, and it sure as hell wasn't gonna be my mother. She could barely take care of herself, let alone her kids.

But life don't wait around for your little science projects, with their solar system dioramas that made us look like we hardly even existed in those unventured outer limits, and the ever- unforgettable lunchroom loony hour with all its food fighting insanity when rent's due, and the fridge is empty.

So yeah, I dropped out. Big whooping deal. Go ahead, judge me all you like, Im all ears! Tell me how stupid I am! Go on! Tell me how I'm just a good-for-nothing, loafing oaf! I dare you, anything you say isn't new to me, I've already heard every damn preachy lashings before over and over. God, it drives me crazy–I just wanna be dumb, deaf, and blind sometimes. Tell me that education is the key to success, and I won't get anywhere without it. The thing is, I didn't seem to get anywhere with it. I was hungrier, poorer, and lonelier. Education is just a distraction from what really matters. It doesn't prepare you for jackshit! It just tells you how screwed you are. Like, is algebra gonna help you out when you've got a gun pointed at 'chu?

Everything I could earn got us outta pickles whenever my mom didn't have enough–but we were already well deep enough into the pickle barrel. I didn't know where she got her portion of the money. I could only guess that Aunt Rosa's inheritance kept her supply rolling in green.

Part of me had figured out that the well dried up a while ago. I didn't wanna think too hard on how else she might've scrounged it up. It'd be too damn depressing.

You'd think I'd be working in the coal mines like way back when. I'm damn near surprised I still got all my ten fingers and toes intact with all the jobs I bust my hump on. A mother unwilling to be a mother, a father abandoning a family he started, now a brother on the cusp of death itself. It all just swelled up at once–like it was about ready to erupt. Like a goddamn pimple ripe for a good gooey burst.

"EVERYTHING is wrong!" I screamed. Gosh, it just came out without any thought. Just as I was about to leave with my invisible tail between my legs, hell, I might as well have had a tail, an old man scuttled toward the driver and whispered in his ear. He had bushy eyebrows that matched his mustache, both silvered and unkempt. A long trench coat hung off his lantern-like frame, the hem stiff like he was. A fedora sat on his head, barely keeping his wispy hair in place. I couldn't understand what they were talking about; it took a long minute or two before they nodded and looked at me. "Why didn't you tell me in the first place?" the bus driver asked.

"Tell you what?"

"That your gramps had been waiting for you!" "He… He was?"

The old man just chuckled and pulled me away from the door. "I am! Come, my boy!" I didn't know what this old coot was talking about as he pointed me to the seat next to him. Was it possibly kindness? I didn't even know kindness was a thing–or if it was, how to show thanks. Hell, I wouldn't even know how to begin if I even could. But again, I heard these tales from neighbors who knew someone who knew somebody else, where these creepo pervs pick out the kid from the litter at the local park they wanna mess with, pretending to be nice. All smiles. God. You ever see someone smile and just know it's all wrong? If you ever see a stranger smile–just run. It's like they want you to trust them, so they slap on a slick salesman grin. But it's all bullshit. It really is. I mean, that's how Mom and Bill became a couple–through a stupid smile. I hate it when people smile at me. Hate it. Then–BAM–they drag you into some dingy alley when your back's turned and enjoy the screams no one else can hear. Not one damn thing. We always got the scoop and stories from our nosy neighbors. Hell, someone's privacy was everyone's affair out on the street. Like little Jenny Baser and her cozy little ride home in her tutor's clunker of a car–everyone knew when they came, with the car's bumper scraping behind, sparking up the street like sparklers whizzing off on the Fourth of July. Sure, that may sound harmless, but when she comes back at eleven, something's fishy. Like, what kid is up that late anyway, and doing what? You'd think it was prime-time, the way folks leaned out their windows, whispering like it wasn't loud as hell. Damn, who needs a TV when the street's got loads of stories you could ever want?

We were on a bus, though–packed with loads of people–so that couldn't happen here, right? Right?

I dragged my feet behind him, almost tripping–the bus was packed. I was wiping my nose with my windbreaker as I sat down, keeping my eyes alert. It killed me when I saw all those God- awful glares from the passengers aboard, all eyeballin' at me as if I were an animal at the zoo.

"Pay them no heed." The old man brushed them aside, patting me on my shoulder, as the bus drove off.

But that was the thing—I couldn't shake their stares, I was going stark raving mad. It was like they were undressing me and taking snapshots for one of them kooky galleries. Every inch in me just wanted to slug each and every one of those snobby pricks, so they would really have a souvenir to make them frown, but that'll just have me be kicked out of the bus, so I dove right into my imagination making a huge splash and socked each and every one of them and boy, did I need that, that made me laugh, it made me laugh so hard I felt like was gonna spill my guts all over, but I didn't thankfully, I didn't want draw any more eyes.

Then, I started noticing the others. Others who didn't stare at me. Im not gonna lie, it damn drove me crazy seeing how miserable each one of them poor saps looks. More pathetic than the next.

There was this guy and his gal, all dolled up with their Sunday duds, newlyweds, I think, who were fighting over a disastrous wedding. See, now, that's what I mean when I say some people trap themselves in hell before hell comes knocking, it's like you invited yourself in. I don't believe in all that wedding bull; it never plays out the way it should. It never does. But again it all starts with that damn smile. Like a warning label, powdered up in sugar. If I ever get hit by Cupid's arrow, God forbid, man, that last thing I want is to go all googly-eyed and goofy- looking, I mean don't you just hate it when your friends with a girl for so long then when you grow up you get those nauseating feelings, And if she's into you, you're probably not into her, or vice versa. So the friendship crashes. And if you do like each other and go out, it crashes anyway, just slower, and you end up looking stupid, wishing you were dead, right back at the start. So why try in the first place?

Love, in essence, is a losing game! What's worse yet is I hate when people try to hook you up, look I may be thirteen, almost fourteen, but I've already had my fair share of dates mostly set ups from the neighbors, and I felt I had to do it, it would prove I was somehow normal, if that's even a thing, to socialize with the opposite sex. Then, when you come back, they're all giddy with excitement, it's like, do they expect you to be a father or a husband after the date? Like my lousy date with teeny Tina the Twig—at least that's what I called her—I dunno, I think it suited her just fine. I get it, I get it, it sounds mean and cruel, but I need some way of remembering her.

And i don't give a crap what any of you think. You didn't have to deal with her! She was too lanky for her own good, really, she was. God, nothing she wore fit right–she looked like a string bean no matter what she had on. She was just... too petite, y'know? Had to wear one of those goofy babydoll dresses, just to look, I don't know, less like a broomstick or something. Even then, she still looked like? Like? I got it! Like a weed blowin' in the wind or whatever. Real brittle, too. One o' those girls, like who'd blow apart if they sneezed too hard. They should always come with a big red stamp that says FRAGILE–DO NOT TOUCH. Boy, and her mouth? Laid out with train tracks. But what really drove me mad was she was always chewing gum it always led up to the nasty strip getting stuck and stretch way too damn far across those metal bars on her teeth– like she was tryin' to replicate the Golden Gate Bridge or whatever. I swear, you'd think she was tryin' to set a world record for building a mouth bridge or something. "Come see the girl with the incredible golden bridge in her mouth," or some junk like that. And she kept pickin' at it like it was the damn beehive. It made me sick, it really did. I couldn't stand it.

It was a date I'll never forget. Tina was wearing this bright yellow dress, the kind you'd see in an Easter parade. She had a red bow tied to her curly blonde clump of hair–if you could even call it hair. To me, it looked more like a crow's nest. A real tangled mess. Another reason why she looked like a twig.

God, I hate the color yellow, I always have and probably always will. It's real depressing. It's way too bright–damn near obnoxious. It's one of those colors that's supposed to make you feel good, but really just makes you want to spew. It's like it was made to brighten days that should've just stayed grey. It's one of those colors that seem to do you a favor just by existing, but it feels so goddamn forced–like it crams itself down your throat and wants you to choke on its cruddy cheeriness.

Don't get me wrong–sunny days are fine, and I'm not one of those drips who want gloomy weather. That gets boring. It's not that I hate sunshine. But does everything have to be rainbows and all that crap, all the damn time?

And the way she kept digging up her nose and eating her boogers–God, it was like she enjoyed that more than the actual hamburger that she barely took a bite of. Hell, that was the worst five bucks I ever spent. I could've used that on someone who at least wouldn't gross me out.

And the worst part? We were splitting a strawberry milkshake. On her request, of course, she wanted to be romantic or something. But how can you go about being romantic with someone who thinks her boogers are part of a gourmet menu?

Screw that. And boy, her conversations were anything but conversational–I couldn't get a damn word in. It was all her. She talked my ear off, just ranting and raving about her older sisters and how they were these perfect goddesses. Guys were drooling over their toes–they'd practically needed umbrellas just to keep 'em dry. She just kept jabbering on and on about how they had the "right curves and angles," like that's supposed to mean something to me. And she kept going– called herself a paperclip, like she didn't deserve to belong in the same room as them, or breathe the same air they did, it was real depressing. I didn't give a damn. I really didn't. And it got to a point where I just snapped and told her to shut up. Just like that. And man, did she cry. She made our business everyone's business in that burger joint–boy, did that tick me off. I swear she drew in a crowd that not even a daredevil stuffed in a cannon, ready to shoot him out through a fiery ring, could've pulled. It was like I'd smacked her straight across the face, and she stormed off. I was hoping that was the end of it, I could pay the tab and go home, but nope, why would it be that easy? Before I knew it, she was back inside, all mad at me for not running after her like some kinda hero wearing a cape or whatever they wear. Like, seriously? Give me a break. So that was that. End of story.

That was the last time I let anyone set me up. Love? Forget it. Cupid can take that stupid arrow and shove it. What is love really? I mean, true love? Is it a warm chocolate chip cookie? Not the cruddy kind you go out and buy that taste like chalk and regret that you scarf the whole damn box before you make it home. No, love can't be bought or at least it shouldn't be, if you're buying love you doin' something all wrong. Love has to be made by tender hands, it shouldn't be all hard and crumbly, it should be soft in the middle, gooey even, like it doesn't care if it falls apart on you, 'cause it knows you'll gobble it up anyhow. That's love. Maybe. I don't know, maybe it's my stomach talkin' and I'm just nuts letting it. But people don't want that. They want all that stiff, showy crap. You go all out, the full nine yards, pleasing the unpleasable with fancy dinners, and diamond rings, and soon handwritten vows where they lie through their teeth about 'forever.' I hate that word forever; nobody actually means it. It's just an overused, tacky bandage that people like to toss around so goddamn much to make themselves feel good because they sprout feathers and cluck like the chickens they are, too yellow or even arrogant to ever admit they'll be gone by Christmas. Like, don't you just hate when a flick wraps up with this cheesy solemn swear to "forever love you, my dear", then the credits roll, but what they don't tell ya is what happens after the credits? A happy ever after my ass! No finales are ever how they actually are or should be; they don't even bother showing the ugly side of it. It's like it's not worthy enough to be onscreen. There is no ride off to the sunset. No star-crossed lover, please, just forget about it. That's just a fancy way of saying 'these two had zero chance from the get-go, but let's romanticize the wreckage anyway because we got dough to rake in. Let's not forget the ever classic, the war is over, and all the soldiers come marching back home, eager to start a family.

Those aren't endings, those are just lame-O bails sprinkled with enough magic glitter to hypnotize the suckers in the audience.

Sure, I enjoy movies as much as the next guy does, if not more. Hell im always at them pictures, but it's just those cruddy endings that get me all riled up its like they're just begging me to punch through the damn screen or better yet, burn the reel with those lousy endings and start fresh. I can't help but feel let down by the way things wrap up, but again, I'm never surprised by them, and they're forever happy after façade. Forever happy after? Yeah, right. More like forever full of shit.

I wanna rip those endings apart, set 'em on fire, and write my own—endings that don't pretend everything's perfect, that show the real mess underneath. Because after the credits roll, that's when the stories get really interesting—that's the crap they don't bother to show you.

So I always end up thinking, after the pictures, do the characters actually mean any of that bull they say about love, about a forever bond, or whatever? Of course they don't because the new showing starts, and again it's the same dilemma over and over again until the credits pop on screen. There is never a definite closing, no reunion, no anything. What happens after the big send off? Do they just disappear, never to have any new adventures again? Do they? I don't have the patience to watch the same damn movie twice. No matter how many times I try to rewrite the ending in my head, it never changes. Forever unresolved.

At least a warm cookie doesn't lie to you like them forever movie endings do. It's just there, warm and small and real. You eat it, and maybe, for a couple of seconds, everything's okay. That's more than you get from most people.

So yeah, if that's love—if that cookie feeling is what we're all chasing—then I guess I get it. I just don't think it lasts, especially forever. Even warm cookies go cold if you don't eat 'em quick. Then they're just leftovers. And everyone knows leftovers get thrown out. Just like everything else.

If love's anything like Twiggy Tina with her train tracks and her booger buffet—then to hell with it. I'd rather shack up alone in some crummy cabin with a pack of mutts that'll rip apart any sucker who gets too close.

By the time I stopped thinking of Tina, the old geezer next to me opened a leather folder and started studying the notes on the page. They looked familiar–like the sheet music I used to see my mom play on the piano back when things seemed better. Real. Alive. Until she pawned it off just to pay off her mounting debts. The music, the joy, the love–all of it stopped. God knows what for; there was never anything in our apartment anyway.

Ever since then, I can't stand music. I'd even throw in–I downright hate it. Whenever a tune started blaring on the radio, I had to hold myself back just from smashing it to smithereens. I hardly know why I wanted to. Still want to. I guess I'm just nuts that way.

To think how easy it must've felt–to just give the piano away like that, with all the memories in it. Like it meant jackshit. That really hurts. Like real bad. Maybe it meant nothing. But it brought us together. Even if just for a second, it felt like something. It felt real. It felt like something that mattered.

Isn't that what we live for?

For something that matters, I mean.

The old man waved his index finger to some invisible melody while humming a few repetitive bars. I started humming along as he turned to me with surprise. Hell, I was just as surprised by it, too, but that single spark made me think of better times.

"You know this song? Do you play?"

"Just listen, I'm not too good at anything. You?"

"I conduct!" he declared, tapping the folder with a crooked smile, like it meant something holy. "If this bus wasn't so slow, I would be at my rehearsal by now. I am already an hour late!"

I figured so, he looked like the blowhard type, the way he went on braggin' about himself, like a real hotshot. He was nothing more than a real pretentious glory hound, a real creepo taking the bows on the backs of the real talent, hogging the spotlight. Then, after, when the curtain falls, he goes on hollering at the kids that made his name worth a damn–kids who could actually play the instruments that he never could. Kids with more talent in their pinkies than he ever had.

That's why he bosses 'em around–makes him feel all important.

There was another face–this kid on the bus–a little girl, probably not much older than Alvin, if that. She was sitting all by herself, one shoe missing, and crying like nobody was gonna hear her. She had this raggedy old doll, missing an eye and all cracked up, clutched in her arms like it was the only thing left in the world

Something about her stopped me cold. I had to find out what was wrong, hoping I could cheer her up. It might sound dumb, but I hate seeing kids look so beat down and sad. They shouldn't have to know that feeling–that crap's for grownups. Kids should be yelling about ice cream or cartoons or fighting over whose turn it is to slide down the slide, not sittin' there like the world already chewed 'em up and spit 'em out. It ain't right. They shouldn't look like munchkin miners crawlin' outta the rubble with no song, no yellow brick road to lead 'em outta the icky mess the grown-ups left behind. There ain't no wizard on the other side waiting to grant every dream.

And that's a damn shame too, kids should dream, 'cause everyone knows you don't got time for dreamin' when you grow up. So dream now, kids, while you still got the chance, and hold onto them good, Lord knows I lost mine. It's like watchin' a balloon that never even got a chance to float–just stuck there, waitin' to pop before it even left the ground.

I'm different. I don't got the time, or dare I say the fantasy, to be happy-go-lucky. I don't consider myself a kid. I gotta wear them adult shoes–size thirteen.

I crouched down and asked gently, "Are you okay? Where are your parents?"

She looked at me, then back at her doll, like she was searching it for an answer. She kept brushing her hair, yanking out long strands with each stroke. Until the doll eventually went bald and its hair formed in clumps around her feet as if we were in a barbershop. I didn't press her.

What would I even say? I just sat there with her for a second. Then she turned to me, holding the creepy doll in front of her face, as if the doll held her voice ransom. "Don't know," she said, her voice all gravelly and weird, like the damn doll was the one talkin. What was worse, she started rubbing that creepy dolly mitt on my arm, that damn thing had no finger, not a single one. "Say, mister, do you got a piece of candy?"

"No."

"Well, I do, look!" She blurted, yanking a piece of taffy from her pocket. It looked like a damn band-aid, all stuck with lint and crumbs and whatever else had been rolling around in there. She held it like it was gold, waving it like the last candy in existence. The funny thing was it was the same taffy Alvin went nuts for, I could just smell the tooth rot.

"That's nice." I managed to say.

"Can-dy's... yum-my... but... don't eat too much... or..."

She drifted off, her words slow and slurred. Her fingers went to her hair, poking and ruffling like she was trying to catch something. Then with a sudden bolt of energy, she exclaimed with a tremoring force "Bugsss... come... see..." but just as quick as she said it, she was spaced out, her eyes half-closed, like she was somewhere else– expecting me to float with her.

"See these creepy crawlies? They're my friends." "There's nothing there!"

"Liar!" she shrieked like I'd just stolen the best present on her birthday. It was damn loud, too, like those announcers in a wrestling match. It was real crummy. I thought I needed to get checked in–but that kid was way crazier than me. I bet she just got dumped off in Lost and Found–and she definitely should've stayed there! I hid my face with my cap and avoided all the passengers who I heard mumble about me. The bus rolled into a part of town I didn't recognize–hell, I didn't care where I was, as long as I was off that damn ride, I just about had enough of this circus on wheels! I just wanted out, y'know? That little dopey girl kept creeping me out. What's worse is that after making a big spectacle of herself, she continued to bug me like mad, whacking me with her doll. No matter where I changed my seat, she would be right behind me. She was using me as a personal punching bag. It was like playing musical chairs. I couldn't deck her, even though I had wanted to. I tried not to as I went on grinding my teeth, keeping my cool. I just sat there and took it, boy did I feel like a sucker. I was swapping seats all over this bum of a bumpy ride, hopping from seat to lousy seat and of course the passengers couldn't keep them peepers to themselves. No one did a damn thing. Not a peep. Bunch of drips, all of them, acting like I was the lunatic. So when the bus finally screeched to a stop, I didn't care where we were–I bolted. There was no chance in hell I was going to sit there any longer and find out what other crazies were onboard. I needed out from the noises, the people, their eyes, their awful stares, from all this madness. I could see myself becoming a shut-in, and for the first time, I understood why Mom left the world to itself, but someone had to be out there–for the family's sake; it had all fallen on my lap, lucky m

After getting off the bus, I didn't have a clue where the hell I was. Nothing looked normal, and just as I was about to ask the driver for directions to the pharmacy, the damn bus took off like a rocket blasting toward the moon–just like it just wanted to shit me out, leaving me stranded. I just stood there for a minute, watching the damn thing shrink into the smog, wondering what kind of world lets kids carry around broken dolls and be wandering alone. I had a reason to, but man, no reason for the girl to be alone was good enough, and it didn't sit well with me. She was younger than me, you'd think somebody, anybody, just one person would care. I couldn't dwell on it anymore, I started walking–cause hell, what else was I gonna do? The street was deserted. Not a car in sight, not even a rusted junker parked along the curb. Just me, the cracked sidewalk, and the kind of quiet that doesn't sit right.

Then, just as I hit the corner of West 52nd, a burst of laughter ripped through the quiet–sharp, loud, mean–like a pack of hyenas from some late-night wildlife show I'd seen. And it was close enough to make me freeze. Boy, what a mistake that was, I shoulda just kept going, but of course curiosity always got the better of me and I stayed a little longer than I shoulda. My legs just gave out–no idea why. They just did, and my eyes darted directly toward the sound of laughter and the shatters of glass bottles, a shiver crawling down my spine. "Great, just my luck to be stuck here when the trouble starts." I found myself saying, or rather groaning, more bull I have to deal with, with hardly any time left, if any, as far as I could dreadfully imagine, Alvin's already dead and buried. That is what scared me most of all, an innocent light dimming that shouldn't be. Just as I got up, a rabble-rousing gang of hoodlums swooped in from just behind a lamp post; there were twelve of them. All dressed in bomber jackets, their collars popped, cuffed slacks, and red caps. The youngest of the bunch seemed as old as me. Their leader? Too old to be the kind of guy boys follow around like pups, especially with that rough moustache of his–patchy and not quite grown in, it looks like a cat's whisker, and when I say whisker mean just one whisker.

The rest of them were just a blur of faces–a bunch of faceless mugs, all mashed together shoulder to shoulder like some jumbled jigsaw puzzle. I felt like I was the only one with a face, it was more than creepy, it was downright screwy, it was as if the whole damn city went awol and I was only one yapping like a busted radio–no broadcast, just static whizzing down the dead street. But the worst part? Anything I tried to say just fell flat as if my mouth was glued shut or something. But their eyes–those damned eyes–glowed red as stop lights. Not one blinked. Not one looked away. I know what I saw. I swear to it. I don't care what anyone says. I know what I saw.

"Say, kid, what the hell you doin' around here? You lost or something?" the leader said, walking toward me… no, floating toward me!

"Where you headed, squirt?"

I didn't say a word, I started backing away. Hell, I didn't know how to fight, I mean sure, I got myself into some scraps before, mostly with punks that messed with Alvin. Before I knew it, I was flat on my face with a busted nose and with Alvin out cold… I couldn't say anything. Thing is, whenever we came back home, all bruised and bloody, boy, Alvin would spin these wild ass stories full of glorious bullshit–and everyone knew it was pure bullshit, too. He was always hyping up his stories, especially when it came to me. He'd brag that I knocked every last one of them out, like I was some kind of badass or something. It got real damn depressing, you know? I mean that I couldn't live up to his fantasized version of me. It didn't cheer me up–if anything, I just got sadder more as he kept on yapping on and on. God, that kid's always up in the clouds, but hell, I can't really blame him. You gotta admit, the stuff you make up sure sounds better than the real crap. So good for him, I guess–wish I could be that dumb sometimes. But I hate how kids grow up and lose that knack for seeing things differently, you know? Like how their dreams get smashed to bits. Nothing's worse than that. It was only a matter of time that a schmuck would come by and barge into Alvin's fantasy land, hell I tried to keep them gutter rats away, but I couldn't do it all the time, it gets tiring, it's just too much damn work

"What's the matter, cat's got your tongue, I can fix that, ya know!"

Just before I could answer, I heard a CLICK of a knife as he started shining his switchblade into my eyes. The flash of the knife ripped my eyes apart, I couldn't see for jackshit. Just white, like I was staring at the sun for hours as if it was blazing just a few feet away, then black. I could only hear their maniacal laughs circling me like vultures ready to pick me apart. Then nothing.

Just… gone. The glare, the knife, and the gang had vanished with the return of my vision. I was on my feet, barely holding myself up, trying to figure out what the hell happened. And if 'lucky' was even the right word for it. But I believed in luck as much as I believed in wishes.

Instead, I saw a group of four bums pawing through a garbage can. I crept past them as if I was some kind of dopey spy in those movies I took Alvin to see as we snuck into the theaters– trying to stay outta trouble, but trouble always finds me no matter how quiet I try to be. So I expect the worst–at least then I won't be surprised. I hugged the wall for my dear life, praying to hell they wouldn't spot me. And they didn't, not at first, but of course, with the Almighty's crummy intervention, they immediately whiffed me out, as I saw them pulling out empty medication bottles from their pockets. They all looked beat to shit, their faces were smeared by dirt and sludge like they have bathing in sewage, long shaggy beards hung from their chins, their ratty suits were shredded, and their hats were filled with holes as if they were used for target practice. I just couldn't get my eyes off of them it seemed as though they all transformed into Bill, scooping up scraps from the bottom of the barrel, being someplace where only the misfortunate gain pardon and brood in sheltered isolation, as they sit and rot waiting for judgement day, whenever and whatever that is. It was the last thing I wanted to think, but in those bums I could just see my bum of a so-called father. I could only laugh at the possibility of them being his pals, because these moochers were exactly the kind of strays that louse would bring home when he used to live with us, hell it took at least two damn weeks for my mom to get the nerve to shoo them away. For a second, I couldn't stop picturing my old man standing with them, scraping for scraps. I nearly laughed. Not because it was funny–far from it, because of the downright likelihood.

"Say, kid, you got some stuff?" a bum called out to me, "Kids like you always got somethin'." he gurgled and smirked. I looked down at my feet, trying to ignore all their blasted hollering. Just as I hit the corner passing them, their smell was deadly; it smelled as though they were camped out in an old, stinking fish market. One of the four grabbed me by the shoulder.

"Didn't you hear him?" the Bum whispered, man, his breath reeked, I swear I almost passed out. Without a second to spare, he lifted me up and started shaking me. "We need it, we need it!"

"What are you talking about?... I don't have anything."

"Give it here!" they all shouted, and man, it was beyond nuts. Like they'd snapped, they dug their hands into pockets like rabid raccoons ransacking a picnic basket–only I was the damn basket.

"It's under his hat, under 'is hat!" A bum snatched off my hat and shook it, hoping anything might tumble.

"Give it back, give it back!" I shouted, but the bums all laughed as they dropped me to the ground. They kept playing keep away while I crawled on the ground toward their ankles. They kept on stomping the shit outta me. Then I got really ticked off, I was no one's pushover, hell, I may get knocked down, but I'm never one to stay down. So I went flying to the nearest bum and sank my teeth into him, hard. Real hard. Like a raving mutt. The taste of his flesh was just damn disgusting, he tasted like curdled milk and someone else's puke, I didn't even care. Hell, I completely lost my mind. I felt I like I could tear his damn throat out, and I really tried. Well I tell ya those lousy bums got real scared and fast, and I couldn't tell if they'd piss themselves because their pants were already soaked. Either way, they weren't so tough anymore. I clung to the guy as he was trying to shake me off as if I was at a rodeo–thrashing around like some wild bronco, I just held on tighter. I bit harder, God I don't how them vampires do this shit, I ain't got the stomach Dracula's got. I think if were to become a vampire, I'd go for straight-up cherry soda or something.

"Take it take it!" the bum cried out, dropping the hat as the other two scamper into a backwash alley, a crackhead paradise. I let go and fell to the ground and watched them digging around the garbage. And again–it just took over in a zap. I don't know what the hell is wrong with me, why I see the crap that I do. Half the time, I feel like some screwball bastard who flushed his meds down the toilet, seeing all this junk, like I'm hooked on a killer dose of some crazy Go-Go juice. The worst part is, I can't even tell if it's real or not... not anymore. And, frankly, I stopped caring ages ago–I just enjoy the whole wacky fiasco.

I saw this massive, disgusting creature claw–like the kind you'd see in some crummy and corny horror flick–come ripping out from inside the garbage can itself. I'm not kidding. It was wet and slimy, looked like it'd been stewing in sewage. Then, just like that, it snatched those sorry saps by their mangled faces and clamped down real hard–then, in the blink of an eye, ferried 'em straight down into the can. It started shaking like real crazy, a washing machine, rumbling with rocks, making this awful, bone-crunching noise–like it was chewing them up. It rattled and belched, as the lid flew up and landed on the street, accompanied by some bones that rolled right to the tips of my shoes, and that was that.

I stood up, brushing dirt off my sleeve, and that's when I saw it as a green flicker caught my eye, the pharmacy. Across the street, tucked between a dead pizzeria called "Bruno's Pies"– with Do Not Cross tape slapped across the door like someone'd gotten themselves killed in there–it looked condemned, easy. Busted windows, all boarded up with rotting wood and crooked nails. Hell, I wouldn't be surprised if there were actual skeletons in there. Literally. Bruno must've had quite a temper. Complain about a pie and you get thrown into the oven, Hansel and Gretel style. I could only guess he must be half-nuts at least. Those odd, sunburned pictures of old buildings were displayed in the dusty window. Odd songs and sounds emanated from the side alley of his joint. It smelled like a kitchen alley. I caught sight of a huge guy in a dirty, oil-stained apron who stared at me when I walked by. "Eh, bambino..eh!" He gestured to me to look in his window while he fanned himself right out there in the street...sheesh..I wanted to run in the other direction. As I passed the alleyway,

I heard his deep laughter behind me.

Talking in another language, nah, not talking, shouting. Never heard it before, and it sounded scary, whatever it was.

And then there was this sad excuse for a pawn shop–the kind of crappy dive with a nasty smell of sex and drugs but without the rock n roll. "WE BUY GOLD" signs are plastered everywhere. What a joke. Like anyone around here was lucky enough to have any… fat chance. The oversized broker in the stuffed and torn chair at the entry was a sight. He was obsessively reading the newspaper as he kept on swearing under his breath as he went on puffing a stale stogie. I wiped the dust off the grimy window and looked through. Antique rifles lined up in one corner, probably busted. Weird oddities and knickknacks filled the cramped space, hell the clutter made the pawnshop looked like my grandmother's house, but at a second glimpse I bet it's my grandma's shit.

These places are most likely haunted, too, it's a damn adoption center, if you really think about it. I'll put money on that too, to spice it up. You bring a precious piece home, and you get a free roommate–what a bargain! Won't pay rent, hogs the bathroom, jacks up the electric bill with their creepy obsession with light –just clicks it on and off all night just for the hell of it. I don't know– my mom wouldn't've freaked about a bought and brought boo- ghost but she'd've gone apeshit over the damn bill. Moves your stuff just to mess with you. They probably have weird ass name too, the kind of dopey name you know a ghost would be stuck with for eternity, because let's face it normal people with normal names like Sandy or Mark, never seem to become ghosts, that luxury is only reserved to the special ones like Dolly or Delbert, I bet it's a Delbert! God forbid you get a lonely ghost–the kind that keeps you up all night, knocking like some goddamn Morse code. Torn furniture was badly patched up with duct tape, and selling it for more than they are worth, anything for a penny, am I right? No dignity.

I swear, it looked like the cats moved in first. Scratched it up, pissed on it, made it theirs. Then, some dope tried gussying it up and called it vintage. You could sell anything to the right sucker if you talk the talk. Doesn't matter what it is–busted junk, fake crap, whatever. Say a few magic words and presto–they're handing over cash like it's holy. Then they invite all their pals hosting a party and expect some sort of admiration for how much class they have for shelling out for vintage shit 'Look how marvelous I am, I have a 18th blah blah.' Yeah, yeah, I get it you're a pretentious shit. It makes me sick, really, and everything was stacked on top of another like a mountain of junk; it's just a crummy landfill. And a pile of beat-up instruments clustered against the wall like some dope gave up halfway through a lesson and needed fast cash 'cause their Tooth Fairy money never came through. Hell, each one looked like it was worth maybe twenty- five cents–warped, banged up, like some idiot glued them back in all the wrong position after feeding them through a goddamn woodchipper.

"You comin' in or what?" he asked as he turned the page and gnawed his cigar. God, you'd think he was chomping on a big Tootsie Roll, the way he was slobbering all over the damn thing.

I looked a little longer.

"I dunno. Looks kinda… oh I don't know, crappy in there… and I don't got a tetanus shot." I laughed.

The indolent shopkeep spat like a camel on the flagstone step, then blew smoke into my face. "You're a real comedian, ain't 'cha kid, now why don't you beat it before you know how funny I can be."

"Yah, yah I bet you're a real tiger… a real killer!"

The shopkeep groaned and went back to reading grumbling to himself, puffing like mad. He went on bitching about 'kids these days' or some damn thing like that, like I was the root of all the world's evils.

I just couldn't stop glaring at that dope. I pictured him swinging over a pool of hungry sharks snapping at his flailing feet. He was begging me to save his sorry ass–and man, you should've seen him bawl when I walked away. I had the last laugh, and boy, that made me feel good when I heard that big splash.

I locked onto the pharmacy across the street because I was just done fooling around with this deadbeat. I could only think what kind of shit he has to endure from his bitchy wife or his naggy mother, probably both. They probably drive him crazy, I'll bet, and can't live up to their expectations. He likely spends all his time on the stoop to just fade away. He's just another sucker who's just as used and shackled like the crappy items he tries to sell off. I wouldn't be surprised if one day it just gets to him and he just snaps and murders them both, he already has that 'I don't give a hell' look.

If it weren't for that ugly little green sign–half-lit, like even it was ok being all secretive–I would've walked right past it. It was that rundown and shitty. But there it was, in all its shitty glory.

It was as if the angels sang when I saw it–one step closer to getting everything back to alright

Hell, who was I fooling? Nothing's ever what it seems or turns out alright. When I ran up to that pharmacy door, I couldn't have been farther from the truth. Miracles don't exist, and luck? Well, luck is bullshit. The pharmacy door was locked, it damn looked near abandoned, if you ask me. I couldn't believe it, I didn't want to believe it. What kind of place that carries medicine closes before sunset? It was plain out bullshit! I tried as hard as I could to open the door, pulling it with all my strength, but it wouldn't budge. I reverted back to my old undying habit of wishing that somehow it would miraculously open, and Alvin's medicine would be packed and ready to be picked up. But wishing for it to be open wasn't gonna get me in. There was no chance in hell I was gonna let Alvin die. Hell what could I do? In a world where boys like me… like Alvin were tossed aside without concern, where surviving what they dished out to us wasn't even nin our hand of cards–like society had already given up on us before we did. Like they shot our innocence right down, ground up what was left of us, and then climbed right on top of those remains just to get ahead. I fell to my knees just thinking how much I hated my dad, my mom.

Did they try? Did they ever?

I started crying as I pounded on the window with all my might, wishing and for the first time praying somebody was inside and would answer me. I wasn't late. I couldn't have been. I shouldn't have been. Then, through blurry, stinging eyes, I saw it. I saw a brick by the side of the pharmacy just lying there as if that was God's given answer, there was no second to think, there was no second to reason, I needed to get into the pharmacy for Alvin's sake, I NEEDED IN. It was time I made my own luck. My brother, my last tether to keep me sane in this screwy world, to keep me from disappearing, his beauty, his innocence, is what drove me to do what needed to be done, "This is for you!" I muttered, not knowing who I was speaking to, either Alvin or, should I mention, as selfish as I may sound, myself. I picked up that brick, which to me it wasn't, it wasn't just any brick; it was a lifeline, Alvin's lifeline. I hurled it right at the window as the glass exploded into a million tiny pieces, spraying me with its icy shards. The alarm went off–loud as hell–while I was crawling through the broken glass, my bloody hands and knees getting cut up, like some dead pig hooked up on a meat hook. I crawled toward the back, jumped over the counter, and tore through that pharmaceutical joint like time itself was screaming bloody murder–it might as well be. I scanned through every cabinet I ripped open then I spotted Alvin Knox's medication section of but when I jimmied it opened it the medicine that should've been there that my mother told me would be here wasn't, No holy grail of inhalers, no magic cure, there was nothing but damn cobwebs and mice shit, those bastards didn't even fill anything, and mom didn't have the guts to do ANYTHING about it! Did she do right? Having no option left, I resorted to breaking open every cabinet in search of an inhaler, for something that could make Alvin all better. But that was when I heard them, a sound I most feared. The same sound that shakes me to this day. It was a I've heard countless times when my father was escorted back home from his drunken rampages. They weren't just police sirens, but the crackling and popping of radio chatter, like they already got you pegged, it makes a guy feel really awful, a drops to a foot tall.

I ducked into the corner the second I heard several cops step out and walk into the pharmacy. I nearly shit myself. They were talking about a string of robberies–"the fifth one this week," they said.

See what I told you? Miracles, hopes, luck? All bullshit.

See what I told you about miracles, hopes, and luck? All bullshit. And now? Well now I knew damn well I was the poor sap caught in the crossfire of this whole damn cherade. As if I wasn't small enough, I knew I would be a hell of a lot smaller by the time they catch me. I heard them investigate the pharmacy. I was too scared to look up; I didn't want them to see me. I did what I always did when I wanted to become invisible. I shut my eyes as I pulled my aviator cap over my face, I was holding my breath too, my God damn breath I felt like I was drowning. "Im not here, im not here," I mumbled to myself, just hoping I'd wake up from a bad dream and see Alvin all bitten up, snoring right next to me with his foot kicking on my face. And for a moment I thought I had disappeared, poof like Houdini 'cept like Houdini I was still there, but only I didn't seem to know it–then that damn flashlight flared up in my face, it was a damn spotlight, it was as if I was the ringleader in circus and all eyes... every single damn light was on me. A pair of hands pulled up my cap, and I saw half a dozen cops all circling me watching me like I was about to pull a rabbit out of my ass. But any attempt at an explanation fell short.

Honest to God, I tried, I really did. But nothing came out right, there was no use in talking my way out of their... suspicions? No, not suspicion or doubt, their ruthless conviction said it all as if they already penciled me in as a cruddy crook. To them and I guess to everyone including myself I was a screw up, I was caught in a mess that never even should've happened if I'd had just a speck of the stuff other people just take for granted. I was stuck in the worst place, at the worst time, all by myself. No amount of blaming would do the trick, and as much as I want to be, I ain't no magician. Then this crazy idea popped into my head–what if, just IF my mom had planned all of this, the missing medicine, the knowledge of the string of robberies, the hours of the pharmacy, Hell, she could 'a notified the fuzz too. I mean, I don't know if she's some kind of mastermind or anything, but just thinking about it made my stomach turn. Terrified me, honestly, it did. Hell, if I couldn't believe this shit, how would they? But I desperately tried anyhow, as I went about crying to them about all that's happen, my father's drunken arrival and didn't have the decency to stay gone, my mom's breakdown a clear excuse for not helping her son by letting her fears warp her into submission, and how it was up to me to solve an unsolvable quest of sorts, you shoulda seen the way those goons glared at me like I lost my marbles I swear, the way I was going on and on without sparing a single breath, you'd think I belonged in one of those crummy nuthouses–frothing at the mouth, strapped into a damn straitjacket. Real nice, right?

Before I knew it I was hauled back onto my feet, anything I tried to say was subjected to scrutinizing disbelief, it's like I gave my voice away, and I defaulted by saying nothing further not wanting to make fool outta myself, but hell, I was already a fool but without the creepy clown makeup. They didn't hear a damn thing did they even care to? Did they? It was really shitty feelin'–really shitty. And just for a second I knew how my mom felt all these damn years having no control her situation or whatever you wanna call it I didn't want to feel the way my mom did, small and inferior. It was so damn loud and hard I has tried to ignore somehow the obnoxious sound not a regular sound where you could cover your ears, no, far from that. It was personal. It was eating me alive, and it wouldn't fade, in fact it screamed even louder, like it knew I tried to shout it out it didn't have a shred of mercy, not a damn ounce.

It just kept on grinding me down into pulp that drips into the backed-up sewage drain. I was squirming like a real dope as they cuffed me, my pleas and protests, everything fell on deaf ears as if they heard all of the bitching and pleading before by others who committed horrific atrocities I could ever dream up, to them it was routine but for me those cries for help, for someone to understand to reassure that everything will just fine be all too damn real. But they didn't give a damn like how rest didn't I was just another voice lost in the raging tide of voiceless cries. My body was pressed against the police car, I didn't hear damn thing they were sayin, the sirens drowned everything out, and through all that blasted noise, that I though my ear were gonna blowout it felt as if I was underneath a damn chapel bell that was ringing, and that's when I heard him.

I swear I heard Alvin's voice–cracked and desperate–'Save me, Colt. Save me.' I stared at the red flashing lights, and then at my reflection in the window. Didn't even recognize it. God, I wanted to cry so badly, but tears didn't come; my well was too dry. I had the raving urge just to bash my head against the window as hard as I could and let my brain, my lousy thoughts, ooze out of my cracked skull, and maybe then it'd finally shut up in there. Just quiet for once, that'd be nice. Let the bustling world go blank as I am now. I just wanted to sink, but instead of sinking into the depths of the abyss that I'd never crawl out of, I was stuffed in the back of the patrol car. As I was being hauled off to who knows where, Alvin's voice didn't fade, it just screamed at me louder–'Help me, Colt, im dying, im dying!" All that cold numbness I'd been stewing in flipped into raw, frantic desperation. I started screaming like some wild baboon that just realized it's trapped in a crummy zoo after the sedation wore off. I wanted out. I needed out.

That unheard desperation ignited an explosive in me–sent me spiraling straight into this rabid rage. I swear I felt possessed by some conjured demon. I refused to be powerless. I slammed my head against the caged barrier, over and over again, I was losing my goddamn mind –losing it with style, might I add. Between those slams, there were flashes of red–something just so awful, and no matter how many times I tried to close my eyes tight, it just wouldn't disappear. Alvin's funeral. An open casket, and there I was, right next to it as if I was supposed to be cooped inside instead, I would have gladly taken his place. Then–in a heartbeat–he sat up. His eyes were black. Pure black. As he raised a bony finger to point at me, the blackness in his eyes started draining like tar down his skeletal cheeks. I bounced back into throbbing reality, if you can even call it that, when I grasped my head and saw my hand slick in blood. I couldn't see straight, I couldn't think straight, it was red, red, red–flashing in my vision, either from blinking stoplights or my gushing head, I didn't know and didn't care to. Things only got worse when I passed my tenement like a sick punchline from God, and what I saw made me want to tear my hands off the handcuffs and kick open the police car door. There on the stoop was a stretcher, a white cloth covering a small body, Small. Way too small. I knew right away. I swear to you, I knew. I already knew the name, I knew the face, I knew everything I needed to.

I started yelling at the cop driving to drop me off here that my brother needed me, that my mother needed me, someone needed me, screamed bloody murder, but he didn't even flinch. Didn't even look at me. Like I wasn't even there. And I just knew–my kid brother was gone.

Just like that. Just... poof. I tried to hold onto whatever memory I had of him, but they just seemed to flutter away when I saw a little arm flop out of the sheet and dangle there as if it was waving goodbye to me. That was the last thing I needed to see; what was worse, the hand was in a baseball mitt, there was no denying it now, no amount of refusal could fool me.

There's not much I can fill in or remember from there. Nothing worth remembering, honestly. I think my reel's jammed, and maybe it might as well be. No real point in continuing anyhow– I'm damn near sick of talking about it. Time just slips away now–does it even exist anymore? I am trapped where I oughta not be, not knowing how long I will be here for and honestly I don't give a damn. I probably never will.

What sucks is I have nothing better to do than write this junk like I have anything half worth decent thinkin for my notebook, or how I say it, a shitter scribbler: entry number blah… like I really give a damn. God, I've done so many entries you'd think I'm makin' a damn menu by now. There's this real kooky doc–his name escapes me, there no point remembering it anyhow but I really should considering he seems to visit me as if I was his only damn patient–you'd think he'd propose by now and give me a diamond ring like the creepo he is–told me I should 'explore and resolve my tangled web of emotions'… whatever that means. Hell I think he was tryin' to be poetic or whatever he sure did suck at it. With all his gibberish, he might as well trade in his briefcase for bongos and attend some dopey poetry circle! Doctor's orders, my ass.

So yeah, let's just call him Doctor Goodlittle, 'cause he does little good for anything

Apparently, I'm some sorry spider to him–the itsy-bitsy kind, y'know? Crawled up the damn water spout, only to get washed right the hell back down. Real pathetic, huh? God. Doctor my ass, if you ask me, he just a quack, he really is, I won't be surprised if he forces me to do a damn picture book about my "experience" next. God! Won't that be a disaster!

So I'm gonna go out on a limb and toss all you a question to consider–and when I say consider, I mean really chew on it, don't just blow it off:

You ever do everything you think is right–and I mean everything, and still end up up to your ears in deep shit?

You can plug up your nose, zip your lips up real tight all you damn want but you're still stuck in stinking shit. And that's the troubling part, you're stuck and got no damn say in it. It's like you just got drenched in acid rain because no one considered the chance of it, rain that can burn, and shove you out into the cold regardless, wearin' nothin' but your pajamas.

That's the part no one prepares you for. You bust your ass, about ready to go all out and damn near kill yourself trying to do what you think is right, to fix what's wrong in your bugged out world gone topsy-turvy–or at least try to–

stand up for what actually matters, and somehow you still wind up the bad guy. The moustache-twirling villain in some comic strip who spends all his time plotting to nab some humongous shiny jewel from a museum or whatever. Ain't that a kick in the nuts?

Come to think of it, people jabber on and on like they're standin' at the edge of the cliff, wantin' to prove how brave they are with their one foot hangin' off with their eyes shut. It's like a game to them–it's really stupid. Hell, it ain't no game–I don't know who the hell thought it was. It ain't something to do. I already fell. Slipped a long time ago. Hell, not slipped–shoved right off. And the worst part? I'm still fallin'. Just never hit the bottom yet. Sad thing is, I keep lookin' down expecting to see a bottom, but don't. That's the sickening joke. I never do. There's this book I was really hooked on–something about ducks or whatever. And there's one part that really ticked me off about it. That whole bit about standin' in a field of rye, catchin' kids before they fall–like someone's actually there to catch you. Cute idea. Cute ideas don't mean they work. I keep catchin' myself sayin', "Look, Holdie–got any brains in that thinkin' cap of yours? 'Cause you missed one!"

My name's Colt… Colt Knox. Hell, I hate my name. I wish I could pick another one– especially now, of all times. There I go again, just a wishin'. This ain't no confession. Hell, far from it. No one else did their job, so I had to fill their shoes, had their coats to wear. If I need to pay the price for it, so be it. I tried at least. Tried to keep a light from dimming. But like everything else I touch, it fell apart. I admit that. The world isn't for those who dream, who wish, who pray, it's all just bullshit to keep you in check. The system is designed for those who can afford it. They get a golden pass… a pass for their future… for their comfort… for their God damn peace of mind. Everybody talks about their slice of the pie, but when they finally grab it, it's just moldy as hell–they just don't know it yet. I think it's just one big stinking setup. No, I don't think it is–I know! It was manufactured to mess you up right from the get-go. And who we believe in, He ain't home. Doesn't answer no bells, spits out those golden passes to the fortunate ones. People like me? Hell, we get stamped VOID on the ass, and the same damn machine slaps you down with a spank instead of a ready to pick up chime. That golden gate, those ones, they walk so easily through–but for us…it's locked. Always has been. No one dares pick it. No one answers our knocks on it.

The only thing I've learned is I am just another page in the story of a lost boy this city chewed up and spat right out. I have been locked here long enough to forget who I used to be, who I need to be. If I could be someone else, maybe. Maybe some old man with a TV tray watching reruns who falls asleep to a blank screen and gets up to go to bed. Who IS anybody, really? It's a nightmare when you think about it. Hell, when you do get out… what brand new world do you step into? Is it even worth getting out? Kicked out to where from where?

You think the people who're supposed to have your back will be there, right? Nope. They stab you in the back when you ain't lookin' and skedaddle off like nothing happened. Don't they know that they can't break what's already broken? Ask them to fix it? You? Back to the TV. Back to the dancing shadows which are nothing, unreal…

Once I heard a voice while I gazed for a long time at the sun through the bars–how badly I wanted to reach out, to capture the light within my palms and never let go. Why was it my mom's voice? Why not some goofy, zealot of a teacher with a message of hopelessness? But it was my mom's. Her voice crooned in a crystalline, chilling chime that drowned everything out and shook me to my core:

'God never picks up requests. And He sure as hell doesn't around here.'

It's just a shame Alvin didn't see the crappy truth of this crud world by his next birthday. He could not reach that far. He could not be spared. My thesis in the flesh. Tragedy as a brother. He was the one good thing I had–my light in all this darkness. And now…poof… gone, I couldn't even say goodbye to his face. It's probably for the best I didn't either, what would I even say?

Maybe I'd sing him that dumb little song he used to sing–you know, the one about the little birds flying high, watchin' the greens and blues go by. Alvin never cared that I laughed at how corny it was. Or maybe I'd say, 'Don't worry…it gets better… the shining wings you beat will carry you on to a better day?' I guess I would just sit. Sit until his last breath went silent.

Gaze into his sad eyes and close the dull lids myself. Would I say 'Goodnight, sweet prince…yah yah yah' then turn away? No amount of bull would be good enough to hear, not for him… not for me. Same goes for that damn Hummingbird. Sure, it hung around–for a moment.

(Confessions of a Hummingbird is being expanded to a full-size novel.)

In Search of the Missing Pond Monster

by David Kelly

Two people are driving in an old, rusty pickup truck: a young man and a much older woman.

A man's deep voice plays from the speakers.

"You see, just beyond where the cotton, tobacco, and green grass grow...

Past the meadow and fields of corn all in a row...

Around the pond where the frogs and dragonflies play...

Lives the biggest Brummble Beem you ever did see.

For those who don't know what the Brummble Beem is, or have never heard of its legend–look it up, find out. This thing is crazy wild.

Now, whether it's a rumor or fact depends on who you're talking to. Most of what you hear is just talk.

But if you stop by Old Man Willard's house outside Rancher's Peak in Huckleberry County, make a right past the town's one traffic light, down the long, long dirt road, around three winding bends, and through a field full of four-legged munchers... there's a dilapidated, crusty old house that used to be white but is now gray.

Well, you'll need to go past that. Behind the house, several hundred feet or so, past the broken-down, gigantic shed, you'll find another house–so gorgeous and pristine it looks like it belongs on the cover of Vanity Fair.

Stop there and ask for a young set of twins named Red and Blue. Then you might just believe the story is true.

You see, they were only twelve when it happened. They're the only ones who ever survived to tell the tale. And I believe them.

Although time has gone by, both of them tell the same story every single time–whether they're together or apart. It's crazy, really, how detailed every last bit of it is."

(The young man turns off the radio.)

"You probably shouldn't have heard that," he says. "It's just a raggedy old CD that's been stuck in my player for years. Those words don't mean a thing. Just some old fable."

The old woman searches for the right thing to say.

"Well, it can't be too old–it's a CD. And I'm not sure it's a fable either. Every word means something, and I've got some extra time today. Why don't I take you up on that fable and we meander right on over to that old man's humble abode and ask those two young folks? You know, so I can hear the story from the horse's mouth."

"If you sit down with one of' em–or both–I've got to warn you.

This story won't just shock you.

It'll change the way you think.

Forever.

I know, because it changed me."

"I've been looking for a story that'll put my writing career back on the map. Maybe this is it."

"Or maybe everyone will think you're a crazy, wacky lady with a few screws loose. You're the first person I've admitted to knowing the Brummble Beem story. And that's only because you heard my CD by accident. Look, I'll drop you off, but that's it. I'm not hanging around. If they're not home, I'm gone. Call an Uber to get back–if you're still alive afterward."

They both laugh as he makes a sharp left turn onto a road that is nothing more than dirt and gravel.

"Is this it?" she asks, pointing toward a house up ahead.

"Not even close. And I know you're laughing now, but listen–seriously. You don't know what the backwoods are until I drop you off. This is a goddamn highway compared to the road we'll be on in a couple minutes. I'm telling you, you're putting your life on the line just going there. This is some scary-ass shit you're walking into."

The woman thinks for a few seconds and then replies,

"Well, I'm not sure how much life I've got left in me, so I might as well get the shit scared out of me one last time."

All of a sudden, the truck swoops into a marshy wetland. The tires are suddenly immersed in pond water. The engine roars.

They bounce through a small gully and enter a huge field of pumpkins. The shocks must have broken a long time ago—because the metal body of the truck clangs against itself with every pothole hit, sending loud bangs and scrapes into the open air.

"Scared yet? 'Cause this isn't even the half of it. We haven't even reached the alligator quarter yet. If this piece of shit stalls, we're in real trouble." He smirks.

"Once I say I'm gonna do something, I almost always do it." She laughs hysterically. "So yeah, keep'er goin', hoss. No gator ever slowed me down before."

The truck sputters slowly now. He turns left at the end of a long row of corn, and they enter a gully a couple hundred feet long. Alligators walk just feet from the vehicle on both sides, nearly window height. One scrapes the side of the truck with its long claws.

At the end of the gully, the truck turtles out, makes a 90-degree turn, and creeps up a gloomy, narrow driveway toward a house that looks like it's been rickety since the turn of the last century.

"It's in the way back. The way way back. Behind that monstrosity of a shed. You've got to walk the last few hundred yards on your own. If you see anyone, just ask for the twins. They'll know what you want. Oh, and… good knowing ya."

He pulls out his phone, flips the camera to selfie mode, and points it toward his side mirror, snapping a photo.

"For posterity's sake," he says.

"And in case something happens and I get blamed, I've got proof I dropped you off alive."

"Thanks again, Brian. I think," she says through the open window, slamming the truck door shut.

"Last chance to back out! Safe travels, Addilynn," Brian calls as he takes another selfie of her walking away.

"Whatever happens, I'll remember you warned me!"

"You're gonna need it," he mutters to himself as the truck rattles back down the road.

———

Past the house, the driveway ends at a sad excuse for a shed. The roof is half missing, the door barely hanging on.

"Behind the shed," Addilynn whispers to herself, spotting a half-beaten path that snakes around it.

The overgrowth forces her to walk carefully. A prickly bush on the left juts out into the path, pinning her against the old shed. It's at least twice as long as any shed she's ever seen. As she slinks along, the path finally opens up a bit beyond the far end of the structure.

"There's no friggin' way there's a house back here," she mutters. "I swear, if Brian was lying to me—if he made up that CD just to lure me into the woods—he's getting a size-9 hiking boot to the shin."

She winds through a corridor of thick, towering bushes. They're so dense she can't see anything but green on all sides. Then, suddenly, her view clears.

There it is.

A house.

Not just any house—but one of the most picturesque, serene homes she's ever seen.

The porch alone could wrap around an entire city block. The white paint is so fresh it practically sparkles, and the structure towers high above the landscape. Its size stuns her.

"A whole army barracks could fit in there—and then some," she whispers, wishing someone were there to hear her awe.

She turns back toward the path, half-expecting to see Brian, half-worried she might never find her way back.

Then, her gaze drifts upward—and she freezes.

The third floor of the house looks exactly like the top of a lighthouse. A full circle of windows encircles the highest room. For a moment, she imagines standing inside, overlooking the fields and forest.

She steps up to the massive double doors and uses the gold-plated knocker. The echo rings throughout the house and out into the open.

Knock.

Knock.

On the third try, the door creaks open slightly.

No one comes.

No doorbell either.

"Hello?" she calls. "Is anyone home? Hello?"

She walks around the porch, peeking into every window she passes.

Nothing. No sign of life.

Turning back to the cracked door, she takes a deep breath and pushes it open. The scent of wood polish hits her immediately.

Inside, the hardwood floors shine so brightly she swears no one's walked on them in days. The living room furniture is covered in clear plastic. She steps in cautiously, tiptoeing across the glimmering surface.

"Hello? Is anyone here?" she calls again.

She moves into the kitchen.

There's a glass of ice water on the table–and the ice is still intact. A mug of coffee steams softly beside it.

Addilynn's skin prickles.

"Someone's definitely here…"

She reaches for the back door when–

A moan.

Loud. Close.

She freezes. The sound is coming from above.

Quietly, she closes the back door and listens.

Another moan.

Upstairs.

Heart pounding, she tiptoes toward the grand staircase, winding upward like something out of a Victorian mansion. She ascends, gripping the wooden handrail. The moans grow louder.

"Mmmm-bluhh…"

Two different voices, crying out the same unintelligible word.

They're coming from the lighthouse room at the very top.

Addilynn climbs the second staircase slower, careful now. If someone's hurt–or something else is up there–she wants to be ready.

At the top step, she sees a foot–huge, in a red boot–jutting out from behind a massive Victorian couch.

The light pouring through the panoramic windows gives the room an eerie beauty–half sanctuary, half stage set.

She pulls out her phone and starts recording.

Creeping around the far side of the couch, her breath catches in her throat. There, lying sideways and still, is a man–his face partially covered in mesh.

Just then–BANG!

A loud pounding comes from a large red door on the far side of the room.

Addilynn jerks upright. "I thought there were windows all around… How's there a door?"

Confused but determined, she crosses the room, her camera still rolling. She grabs the handle and flings the door open.

Inside–two people. Tied back-to-back, bandanas over their mouths, slumped on the floor.

They both moan.

"Unn-I-uuu… Unn-I-uuu…"

Addilynn throws her phone into her pocket and yanks off the bandanas. First the girl's. Then the boy's.

"What happened?" she demands, even before they can speak.

She drops to her knees, undoing the knots on their hands, which are dark red and purple from lack of circulation.

"Our dad–he was hiding us from the Brummble Beem," the girl gasps. "He said he knew how to fight them off. Have you seen him?"

"I think he's just outside that door," Addilynn replies, untying the last rope.

The two young people spring up and run to the man behind the couch.

"Dad! Are you okay?" the boy shakes him gently.

The girl checks his pulse. "Still breathing."

She leans over and listens for breath.

"Let's get him onto the bed," she says.

"Are you sure you should move him?" Addilynn asks.

"No–but we're doing it anyway. Grab his feet, will ya?"

Together, they lift him and carry him to a bed on the far side of the room.

The girl turns to Addilynn and says, "The name's Red. That's my brother, Blue. And this is our father–Dr. H.W. Willard. He's not much for talking right now... give him a few minutes to warm up." She grins.

"Addilynn Beatrice Clemens," she replies, pausing. "So I've finally found Red and Blue. Not what I expected. May I ask how old you two are?"

"Of course," Blue says.

"Good. A master of semantics. So–how old are you now?"

"Whenever someone adds now to that question," Red says with a smile, "it usually means they've heard the story."

"Fair. I'll admit it–I know what I came here looking for."

"I just turned 22," Red says. "Blue's turning 24 in a couple of months."

Blue focuses on his father, pouring water onto a washcloth and dabbing his forehead and lips.

A few seconds later, Dr. Willard stirs.

"I guess I showed him a thing or two, huh?" he mumbles.

———

"Dad, this is Addilynn. We're not entirely sure why she's here," Blue says, raising an eyebrow toward her.

Dr. Willard sits up, stretching. "My pleasure," he says with a small bow of his head.

"You look a lot better now than when you were unconscious on the floor," Addilynn quips.

"May the compliments keep coming," he replies, gingerly climbing out of bed.

"I'm quite good at stating the obvious," she says. "It's what makes me highly qualified to ask questions with no concern for accuracy."

The doctor chuckles, then tilts his head. "And what, may I ask, brings a stranger so deeply into our humble living quarters?"

"Umm… well, the front door pretty much opened itself. Then I saw the steaming coffee, untouched ice… and then I heard a noise. Which led me up here, to your delightful attic. And then–surprise–your children, tied up, and you passed out cold. Not exactly neighborly."

Red folds her arms. "So, Dad… what happened while we were, um, away?" She air-quotes with her fingers.

Dr. Willard gives Addilynn a look. "Ah, quite the contrary to your thinking, young lady. I didn't abandon them. I risked my own demise–but I also showed that Beemer who's boss."

"Okay," Addilynn interrupts, "maybe we could all sit down with a hot drink–whatever's still warm–and you can walk me through this whole mess. Because right now? I'm more confused than a porcupine at a balloon party."

"Splendid idea," the good doctor says, dusting himself off. "To the kitchen, then."

As they descend the grand staircase, Addilynn turns to the twins.

"If I may ask something a bit forward–are you two actually twins? I was told you are. And have you really met the Brummble Beem?"

Red smirks. "That's not even close to forward. And yes to both. Though I wouldn't exactly use the word met."

They reach the kitchen, and Red immediately busies herself with the coffeemaker.

"Coffee? Tea? Poison of choice?" she asks.

"The usual," Blue blurts out.

"Me too," says Dr. Willard.

"Cold water for me," Addilynn replies. "It's another hot one out there."

She sits down, readying her phone for recording.

"I hope you don't mind if I document this. I've been chasing this story for years."

Red and Blue both nod their consent.

Dr. Willard raises an eyebrow. "Before you grill my fascinating children, might I suggest you explain what you're doing blatantly intruding on our private little life?"

"Fair enough," Addilynn says. "I was hitching a ride with a guy named Brian, headed to Felton Manor. A CD started playing in his truck–the one about the Brummble Beem. And it mentioned your twins. As a writer, I couldn't help myself. So… here I am."

"Well, that certainly checks all the boxes for strange," Dr. Willard replies, sipping his coffee.

Red chuckles. "I've told this story so many times the thrill's worn off. Blue, why don't you start this time?"

Blue takes a breath, nods, and begins.

"Dad had sent us on one of our usual missions. We were coming back from the Wilsons'–just a short walk on the north side of the lake. We shortcut through the swamp to save time. Red had a plastic bag inside her backpack to carry the sugar and flour Rita lent us. Blackberry pies were on the line, so she was serious."

"Let me cut in so we don't turn this into a five-hour epic," Red interjects. "Blue and I were knee-deep in marsh muck when we heard it–a deep, echoing howl. It ripped through the cattails like a chainsaw through silk. We froze. Then Blue grabbed my hand and ran."

"Well, 'ran' might be generous," Blue adds. "It was more like flailing through knee-high goop while screaming internally."

"But then I realized something," Red says. "The Brummble wasn't chasing us. It wanted what was in my bag–the food. Blue was ahead of me, hurling rocks, trying to slow it down. I ripped off my backpack and tossed it."

"The Brummble stopped dead in its tracks," Blue picks up. "It tore the bag apart like a raccoon at a trash buffet. Sugar. Flour. Gone."

"Ugliest thing I've ever seen," Red says. "Tall. Gaunt. Antennas like twigs. Patchy black and gray fur that looked like it had been through ten forest fires and one dog grooming apocalypse."

"It was fast, too," Blue adds. "And the way it moved–like a ballerina with biceps. Freakishly graceful. Also… it kept shielding its eyes. Like the sunlight hurt."

Addilynn raises an eyebrow. "So you think it lives underground?"

"Or in a cave," Blue says. "Or somewhere dark."

"We made it home and screamed for Dad," Red says. "He was outside chopping wood. All three of us bolted into the house and locked everything. But the Brummble never followed."

"That was the only encounter," Blue says. "Until today."

Addilynn leans forward. "So… was it a Bigfoot? Or like the Abominable Snowman?"

Dr. Willard waves a finger. "Don't lump it in with those urban legends. This thing was real. And terrifying. And not alone."

"You mean there's more than one?" Addilynn asks.

Dr. Willard holds up three fingers.

Red nods. "We found three different sets of claw prints days later. Maybe four."

"We agreed not to talk about it publicly," Blue says. "Didn't want to start a panic. Until now…"

Addilynn glances down at her muddy clothes. "So… those footprints you mentioned–can I see them?"

Red snorts. "You won't just get dirty. You'll be head-to-toe mucked."

Blue smirks. "It's a thirty-minute walk around the lake, or a twenty-minute shortcut through the swamp."

"Unless you want to do that alone," Red adds, "you're coming through the lake with us."

Dr. Willard smiles. "They know the land like the backs of their hands. But if it's you or them getting approached by a Brummble…"

"They'll scatter faster than a squirrel in traffic," he finishes with a grin.

"I get the message loud and clear," Addilynn replies, finishing her water.

Red stands. "Let's git a-goin'. Be down in a country second!"

She sprints up the stairs. Dr. Willard leans in to Addilynn.

"They'll be good tour guides. But… they ain't stupid. If danger shows up, expect them to choose life. Quickly."

Addy nods. "Fair enough."

Red flies back down the stairs. "I beat him! I finally beat him!"

Dr. Willard claps. "He'll never live it down."

Blue thumps down a moment later, skipping every other step.

"Let's skeedaddle," Red says, already halfway through the kitchen.

Addilynn rushes after them, the back door slamming shut behind her.

She jogs to keep up, laughing breathlessly. The breeze is cool, but the ground is wet and soft. A splash up ahead lets her know–they're already in the lake.

As she takes her first stride into the murky water, the smell hits her like a wall. Swamp. Stagnant. Rich with decay and secrets.

"Wait up!" she calls.

They both turn, raise a finger to their lips in perfect synchronization, and then keep moving forward–silently–into the marsh.

———

What happened next depends on whom you ask.

All three–Red, Blue, and Addilynn–recall the events differently. But if you average out the chaos, the truth goes something like this:

Red was leading the way through the lake, not ten feet ahead of her brother. One second she was there–the next, she was gone.

Vanished.

No splash. No scream.

Just–gone.

Blue stopped cold. "Red? RED!"

He stood frozen for a beat, staring into the swirling brown water. Then panic set in. He began frantically swiping his arms through the water, slapping the surface, diving his hands downward.

Addilynn, waist-deep in murk, rushed to help.

"She was right in front of me!" Blue shouted, breath heaving. "She was right there!"

They both plunged their hands beneath the surface, digging through the silty muck, hearts pounding.

"Where could she have gone?" Addilynn cried.

No bubbles. No movement. No sign.

"I ain't leaving her!" Blue shouted. "You! Go get Dad! Now!"

Without hesitating, Addilynn turned and waded back toward the shore, screaming Dr. Willard's name before she even left the water.

Blue stayed behind, chest-deep in filth and fear.

Then–

A soft splash.

He spun around.

A smile bloomed on his face so big it nearly cracked him in half.

Red's head surfaced slowly from the muck, like a mythical creature rising from slumber.

"There you are!" Blue shouted. "I was about to lose my damn mind!"

Red coughed, gasped for breath, then laughed.

"Thank goodness you're the reigning breath-holding champ of Huckleberry

County, five years running," Blue said as he hugged her tight.

"Yeah, well, let's hope nobody told Addilynn that," Red grinned. "Because she's probably screaming bloody murder back at the house."

"She'll be fine," Blue said. "Besides, Dad's not even home. He left right after we did–went on a house call to help Jimminy Cravins with a twisted ankle. I know, because I told Jimminy to call right when we left so we'd have the place to ourselves."

Red raised a soaked eyebrow. "Wait. That's the only reason I beat you down the stairs?"

Blue gave a wicked grin.

The two stepped out of the pond, dripping mud from their necks to their socks, and turned left–away from their house.

As they disappeared into the tall grass, the camera of this story pans down–revealing hundreds of strange, deep-set footprints pressed into the ground.

Back at the house...

"Doc! Doc, where are you?!" Addilynn yelled as she burst through the back door, dripping wet.

Silence.

The kitchen, untouched. No sign of him.

She sprinted up the grand staircase. Doors flew open–empty rooms. Nothing.

She found a wooden ramp leading to the third floor, toward the bell tower. At the top, she flung open a heavy window.

Birds scattered as her voice boomed across the land.

"DOCTOR WILLARD!!"

She screamed into the sky so loudly, the trees themselves seemed to flinch.

No reply.

Out of breath and frantic, Addilynn scurried back down to the kitchen and pulled out her phone.

"911," she muttered, pressing the digits.

A strange ringtone buzzed in her ear.

"911 dispatch. What's your emergency?"

"Yes! I–I think there's been a drowning! A girl–Red–she disappeared into a pond. Her brother stayed behind to look, and I came to the house to get their father, but he's… gone!"

"Are you with the person now?" the dispatcher asked.

"No! I told you, she's gone. Underwater!"

"Ma'am, I need your location."

"I don't know the address. It's… it's Dr. H.W. Willard's house. Do you know him?"

"Huckleberry County dispatch. I've never heard of a Doctor Willard."

"What?! That can't be right! What about Red and Blue Willard? Or Addilynn Clemens?"

"Ma'am, I'm going to need a street name."

"I don't know the damn street name! I was dropped off by a guy named Brian in an old truck! I didn't exactly take notes!"

"Is there another house nearby?"

"They said the Wilsons live nearby–but I don't know where. Listen, I've got to go back. I left Blue at the pond. He's alone."

"Ma'am, do you want me to stay on the line–?"

"Maybe you can help when I get there. I don't know. Just–just stay on if you can."

But as Addilynn turned to run out the back door, the call dropped.

The signal was gone.

She dashed back to the lake, phone shoved in her pocket, heart hammering.

"Blue? Red?" she whispered loudly, trying not to attract attention from… anything else.

She reached the water's edge.

Nothing.

No movement.

She thought: Should I go check for footprints? They had mentioned some on the far side of the pond. That might be proof. That might be something.

She pressed forward, stepping into the brown swamp water again.

A howl suddenly erupted behind her.

Deep. Animalistic. And close.

Addy dropped to the ground, clutching her ears.

The air filled with a sickening smell–like a zoo on a summer day mixed with manure and rotting hay.

Shwoop! Shwoop!

Movement. She turned–but the sound stopped.

"What the hell was that?" she whispered, eyes wide.

Then–two more shriek-squeals–less than ten feet away. The cattails shook violently.

Addilynn ducked, heart in her throat. She crawled toward the sound, curiosity overpowering fear.

But before she could get far–Thump!–something shoved her from behind.

She landed face-first in the mud.

Was that... laughter?

As she wiped the filth from her face, she saw them.

Footprints. Hundreds of them.

Different sizes. Deep. Unmistakable.

She blinked.

"This isn't one or two Brummble," she whispered. "It's a whole community."

Realizing she'd wandered far too deep, Addilynn looked around for an exit.

What did Red say?

"The Wilsons' house is just a short walk north–three minutes if you know the way."

I don't know the way, she thought. But I have no better option.

She crawled through the cattails until she spotted a worn trail.

"Please let this lead somewhere…"

As she crested a small ravine, panting and sweating, she saw a modest house up ahead.

Movement on the porch.

She crept forward, hiding behind a large oak tree.

She rubbed her eyes clear. What she saw next froze her blood.

"Those are… Brummble Beems!" she gasped.

Then she blinked.

The porch was empty.

Gone. As if they were never there.

She stepped onto the porch anyway.

The scent of wild horses and fresh-baked pie filled the air.

Just as she reached to knock–

"Addilynn, is it?" said a woman, appearing as if conjured from thin air. "Come on in. I'm Ms. Roberta Jeannie Wilson–but just call me Rita. Don't mind the mess. I've got persimmon pies in the oven that'll burn faster than a scarecrow at a bonfire."

Addilynn stepped into the kitchen–and froze.

At the table, muddy and dripping:

Dr. Willard.

Red.

Blue.

Brian.

Addilynn stared at them, slack-jawed.

Above Brian's head, a wall of photos–people getting out of his truck, each with him snapping a selfie.

He stood, thumbtacked a new photo to the wall–Addilynn's.

"I guess you didn't see this coming, did you?" Red grinned, her voice eerily calm.

As she laughed, two small antennae unfolded from behind her ears.

They weren't props.

They were part of her.

AUTHORS IN BRIEFS

Adam Paterson

My nom de plume is Felix Von Bruder: A seasoned educator and the world's okay-est writer. His first book, What I'm afraid of and Alligators, is an acclaimed hit by his third-grade teacher. His stories feature ordinary people facing absurd and extraordinary events, much like his own life.

Jeffrey Albert

Jeffrey is an educator, lecturer, builder, and writer, now 50 years in the tiger's tech tank, goes AWOL. Buried in the plains of India, the ruins of Mesoamerica, the great halls of China and mountains of Japan, he goes looking for the mystery of it all. The vast confluence of the Kumbha Mela, Shaolin Mt. Wutai, the monasteries and temples of Kobo-sama, the paths of Yoshitsune. He is no one. Now here.

Mark Donnelly, PhD:

Mark is an artist, educator, community activist, Freemason, a proud husband and father of four exceptional adults, and a fierce dreamer. Many believe that the older he gets, the younger his imagination becomes. He is the author of 48 books (and counting), including children's book, books about Western New York, and a series of novelty cookbooks.

Mason Winfield:

Author, researcher, storyteller, and "supernatural historian" Mason Winfield is upstate New York's premier paranormalist. Mason studied English and Classics at Denison University, earned a master's degree in British literature at Boston College, and studied poetry and fiction at SUNY Buffalo with professor emeritus and MacArthur grant recipient Irving Feldman. In his thirteen years at The Gow School (South Wales, NY) he chaired the English department, won a 50K cross-country ski marathon, and was ranked in the Buffalo, NY, area's top ten tennis players.

Ken JP Stuczynski:

Ken is a life artist, author, publisher, Interfaith Minister, and futurist, living with his wife and pets in South Buffalo. He aims to misbehave, get into good trouble, and write a full novel version of "And Then They Were Gone..." on top of his historical and metaphysical projects.

Austin Clark:

Born, raised, and educated in upstate western New York, Austin Clark spent his childhood dreaming of having adventures. Then he grew up and decided to have some. He currently lives in Buffalo, NY - a place he finds both classy and vulgar, which is what any good person, place, or story ought to be.

Avi Albert:

Avi Albert is an author whose writing is deeply rooted in personal experience and an unwavering love for storytelling. Born with cerebral palsy, Avi faced a childhood often overshadowed by physical limitations and the isolation that came with being bedridden for extended periods. From an early age, Avi discovered the power of storytelling as a means of escape. What began as a simple pastime grew into a passion that would shape his life.

David Kelly:

David has been a teacher and coach in the Buffalo Schools for 20+ years. He has two beautiful and dynamic sons, Mason and Zephyr, and is married to the love of his life Mercy, who brings so much energy and pizazz to our family.